The Wishing Race

Colin Fletcher

POOLBEG
FOR CHILDREN

Published by
Poolbeg Press Ltd
123 Baldoyle Industrial Estate
Dublin 13, Ireland
E-mail: poolbeg@iol.ie
www.poolbeg.com

© Colin Fletcher 2000

Copyright for typesetting, layout, design
© Poolbeg Press Ltd

A catalogue record for this book is available from the British Library.

ISBN 1 85371 987 0

Cover design by Artmark
Illustration by Peter Hanan
Printed by The Guernsey Press Ltd,
Vale, Guernsey, Channel Islands.

For my wonderful daughters,
Emma & Sarah

About the author

Colin Fletcher left school when he was fifteen and worked for nine years as an electrician in East Suffolk. When he was twenty-four he moved to Norwich where he trained as a teacher. He taught for twenty-three years in Primary and Middle schools in Suffolk and Norfork. He has now left full-time teaching and spends most of his working week writing for children. He lives alone on the Suffolk coast and has two grown-up daughters. *The Worst Class in the School (1999)* was his first book for Poolbeg.

Contents

1

Sylvia

Saturday 4th March

Sylvia was a prisoner. No way could she ever get free. She was chained to them every single minute – Monster-man and Monster-woman. And this bedroom was just a torture chamber.

"No Daddy!" she screamed as he slammed her history book onto her desk.

"What do you call *this?*" he demanded, about one centimetre from her face. "It's *rubbish,* girl! *Rubbish!*" She could actually *feel* his scratchy beard!

"S-S-Sorry, D-D-Daddy." *Oh, no! Not the stammers again!* She tried a spell-number twenty-seven:

> *From mouth and ear*
> *Stammers disappear!*

"Is *this* the sort of work we should be getting from *our* daughter? *Is it? Is it?*" Spit was beginning to foam from his red lips.

"N-N-No, D-D-Daddy. I-It i-isn't."

> *From mouth and ear*
> *Stammers disappear!*

"YOU CAN DO WONDERFUL WORK, SYLVIA! *WONDERFUL!*"

I can't! I can't! she yelled in her head. *That's only when I cheat! Don't you know that? I cheat! I can't do it!*

"*This* is the sort of work I'd get in from those *estate* kids out there! NOT FROM MY OWN DAUGHTER!" he boomed.

His temper-bomb exploded and his big, open hand flashed towards her face. *Emergency dive!* She sort of ducked down and squiggled out between his legs.

"YA-AH!" he yelled. But he missed her completely and thumped her wardrobe, shaking it and rattling the hangers.

Now she was trapped against it. *Witch eyes!* Try your *witch eyes!* She half-closed her eyelids till he looked all blurred and wobbly and out of shape.

> *Ugly giant, Monster-man,*
> *Become the handsome prince again!*

Please, Daddy! *Please* be nice Daddy again!

"I want this done *again!*" he thundered. "Do you understand?"

Sylvia Witch fails again! "Y-yes, D-Daddy. I w-will."

"Anyway, it's time for maths, now," the torture-master growled, lumping onto her chair.

Maths! Oh, no! My brain will break! Got any new brains Mr Frankenstein? She'd already done her Saturday spellings (copied secretly from her codebreaker notebook)! Her tables (by sliding the answers out under Jemima Puddleduck). That *stupid* writing about the *stupid* Anglo-Saxons. *And* she'd trotted round behind her mother on their daily three-mile run! It *was* torture!

He was sorting out some maths. She could hear children screaming and playing out in the road. He had his back to her. She turned and blinked at the sunny window . . . *Escape! Escape! Dive out of the window! Super Sylvie flies free! Super Sylvie joins the human race!* . . . She was never allowed to go out and play with them. *Never!* She wasn't even allowed to *talk* to them. He probably thought she'd *catch* something from them! But today . . . maybe she could . . . just . . . No! . . . ! *Yes, yes, Sylvie! Go on! Try it!* He can only *execute* you! A firing squad, or something! *Peow!* Sylvia Starr, rest in peace! She threw a glance at him – He still wasn't looking . . . Sylvia the escaping prisoner crept over to the window. Now . . . dare she actually? . . .

She stretched an arm out very slowly . . . and just touched the curtain . . . Then she eased it back the weeniest little bit . . . and looked through the crack.

The world outside was Saturday-morning bright and Saturday-morning happy. The children were jumping up and down in the road. They were smiling – She smiled as well. They were doing a sort of a dance in a ring – her own feet began to skip . . . And, when they held hands, *she* stretched an arm out and clasped imaginary fingers.

Her father, Walter Starr – The children at school called him Stormy Starr – was watching her. He didn't have the control over his feelings that most headmasters have. And sudden thunder raged on his red face again and lightning flashed in his eyes.

"SYLVIA!" he bellowed.

She twisted round. "S-S-Sorry! Oh, I'm s-so s-sorry!" she pleaded.

He marched over and yanked the curtain open so violently it made her shriek. *"These people!"* he sneered, sweeping his arm over the whole estate. "What good are they, eh?" He swung round towards her.

"N-n-no g-g-good, D-Daddy," she answered obediently.

"No good at all!" he spat, looking out again.

They had stopped dancing. They were climbing on shoulders, swaying – building a human tower. They looked nice. Why did he keep her away from them? Even at school!

He turned her towards him with his finger-tips. "You're not like them, Sylvia," he said, looking right into her. "*You* are going to *do something* with your life. *You* are our little brain-box, you are!"

She *wasn't*. She wasn't their little brain-box. She was *hopeless*. Hopeless at everything . . . except cheating him. Pretending. Acting . . . and running, of course, which she hated one million hates!

"Now! Back to work!" he said. "Percentages!"

Percentages! Oh no! She hated percentages *two* million hates! "Oh, I l-love percentages, D-Daddy," she said, sitting down at her desk. She read the first one quickly, trying to get ahead of him. "Find ten per cent of 650" *What in the diddle-poo does that mean?* Her stomach lurched and hands grew damp with fear.

"These should be easy for you," he said behind her. "We did them a few weeks ago, remember?"

"Y-Yes. Y-Yes," she agreed. That was when she'd had that calculator watch and she'd pretended to be scratching her wrist. But she hadn't got it today.

"What do you think?" he asked.

"Oh – easy, easy," she said.

"Right!" he decided. "In your head this time, then! Just give me the answers – Number one?"

In my head? Oh, dash and blow the giant-o! "I . . . Ah . . . W-well . . ." she struggled.

"Come on! Come on!"

She stared at the question. "I-it's . . . I-it's . . ." she faltered.

"I-it's, i-it's WHAT?" he demanded.

"Oh. I-I-I-It's . . ."

"DON'T DO THIS TO ME, SYLVIA!" he roared.

Oh where was her maths god?

"TEN PER CENT IS EASY, CHILD! TEN PER CENT! *TEN PER*

CENT!' Walter Starr, the all-powerful headmaster, was trying to *shout* it into her.

"I-I do know it. I-I'm j-just . . ."

His big fist WHAMMED down on the desk beside her, bouncing Toddy Teddy into the air and scattering her felt tips. She screamed. Froze. Stared at him.

She always had to get to this point – this hopeless, terrified state – before her gods showed her the way out . . . and it came to her like a present arriving in her head. She jumped up, a different person, smiling and confident. "Got you there, Daddy," she joked. "You really thought I couldn't do them, didn't you?"

An uncertain smile flickered on and off his moody face.

"These are easy-peasy, these are!" she said. "Give me some really hard ones, Daddy. Go on. I *am* your little brain-box, aren't I?"

He laughed. "You're always amazing me, Sylvia," he said.

Thank you, God, thank you. Now please, please, please *make them easy!*

"Here!" he said, lifting a book out of his brief-case. "Here's a challenge for you. 'A-Level Number Work'. If you can do these now, at your age, you could be at Cambridge by the time you're sixteen! Cambridge, girl! Think of it!"

She stared at the page. *Suppose you think that's funny, God?* The writing was really tiny. She could hardly *read* it, let alone understand it. She'd *never* be able to do these!

"Manage them?" he asked.

"Oh, y-yes, y-yes! Tell you what. A challenge, Daddy! You and Mummy go to school to get the mail." (Her mother was Deputy-Head at the school)! "And I'll have all these done before you get back! Challenge?"

"Challenge!" he agreed, looking all stirred-up and excited.

She thought he was actually going to *hug* her. And she had that strange feeling again. She wanted him to, *three million wants* but she didn't want him to, *four million wants!* "You get these done – *and correct* – before we get back and . . . and . . ." He scanned his head for a favour . . . "And you can watch half-an-hour's television later!" (Her telly-watching was *strictly* rationed).

* * *

When her father left the room, Sylvia slumped onto her chair. She was *terrified* of him – but she wanted to please him so much. She started to read the first sum for the *third* time: "If you invested one thousand pounds . . ." What's the point? She didn't have a clue! Perhaps she should burn the house down! *Oh dear, Daddy, and I'd done all those percentages for you!*

She wandered over to the huge bay window again – They were both so proud of this house. "It's Georgian. A manor house," they'd told her twenty million times! You could see nothing but fields and woods from this window, once, they said . . . The BMW slid out from under the laurels, down the dark drive . . . and away . . . racing past "all those new, *common*, estate houses" that surrounded them now.

Her eyes fell back on the children. They were staring up at her through the open gates as if she were an alien! Dare she just? . . . *No!* Don't even *think* it! . . . but no-one would know! . . . so she did! She shot her arm up and *waved* to them. And she yelled to them. For the first time in her life! They just jumped away as if she'd bitten them and she laughed. At school they were forbidden to go anywhere near her! She even had her own desk in her own little alcove!

But one girl *did* wave back. A long, wild, crazy wave. Sylvia beamed at her. It was Bernadette – they called her Bernie. She was nice but she was from "that dirty, Gipsy family," as her father called them.

"O-PEN THE WIN-DOW!" Bernie mouthed.

Sylvia laughed again and clapped her hands. She felt all *fizzy* and giggly . . . and a sudden *whoosh* of excitement spun her round and carried her *right out of her bedroom-cage* . . . down the dark-wood stairway . . . past the deep-voiced grandfather clock . . . and *OUT!* Into the sunshine!

2

Sylvia

Saturday 4th March

pShe stood and sucked in some of the lovely bright air for a moment. Then she skipped down the drive as far as the gates . . . and stopped . . . They looked frightened. As if she were a *ghost!* She didn't blame them. Their house *did* look like a gloomy old castle. And people *didn't* usually come running out of it . . . She laughed and danced out to meet them. "I've escaped!" she said.

Bernie's laugh rose and fell like wild music. "I knew you'd come out one day, you!" she sang. She had really long, black hair, all curly. And dark, twinkly eyes. "Rapunzel has come out of her tower!" she told the others.

"Are we allowed to *talk* to her now, then?" the freckled boy, Mopsy, asked.

"*NO!* We'll get *done!*" little Midge warned him.

"Oh yes we are!" Bernie said. "Sylvia's been rescued. She's with us now!" She took hold of Sylivia's arm as if they were a wedding couple.

"Is she hiding or seeking, then?" Mopsy asked.

"Seeking! With me!" Bernie told them. "You lot can hide. We'll give you fifty – One, two . . ."

How had she got out here? It was like a different world. Like she'd gone through that magic wardrobe or something! She felt so, sort of *happy*. Like all her troubles were a million miles away.

* * *

She stayed with Bernie for ages and they did really daft things she'd never done before.

They did a circus act, balancing along someone's garden wall.

They acted out a play about Dracula up an alley-way.

And they did a TV show for the boys: "The *LICE* Girls!" Bernie announced. "The greatest insect sound since *The Beetles!*" Sylvia pulled a really disgusting head-lice face and she heard Bernie's up-and-down laugh again.

> *"If you wanna be my liver,*
> *If you wanna be my brain,"*

they sang . . . The boys cheered and smacked them on their backs. Sylvia loved performing! It made her feel sort of free.

After that they started this nipping war. "Aah! YEOWCH!" Sylvia screamed, hopping about and enjoying it.

A dark blue BMW appeared at the far end of the road. The sun glared off it as it edged slowly towards them.

Sylvia was struck rigid. *Oh, God! Save me! Please!*

"Don't worry, you," Bernie said softly. "You'll be okay with us."

But Sylvia didn't hear.

"You lot!" Bernie commanded the boys. "You hold the car up! I'm taking Sylvia in." Sylvia let herself be dragged by the wrist into their driveway. The gates clanged shut behind them. And the boys began tying them together.

Sylvia would do *anything* to please her parents. She'd never done anything like this before. "Th-they'll k-kill me!" she said, fumbling the door-knob.

Bernie had never seen anyone so frightened. "Why will they?" she asked, slipping in behind her.

"Because I've been with y-you!" she said. "Y-you're dangerous, you are! And I haven't d-done my b-blinking, b-blooming per-per-centages!"

They were in the huge, dark hall. "Show me. Go on. Show me your per-per-percentages," Bernie said. They could hear him outside, roaring at the boys.

Sylvia couldn't *believe* that she'd actually brought the gipsy girl *into their house!* "Y-you'll have to g-go!" she pleaded.

But Bernie just smiled calmly. "Show me those percentages," she insisted.

The car began crunching up the drive and Syliva screamed. She ran up the stairs three at a time. Bernie a long way behind, chuckling.

"H-here!" Sylvia said. "L-look. You'll n-never be able to do th-these!" The book was trembling in her hands.

Bernie pushed her hair back, shuffled herself comfortably on the chair and studied number one.

"H-HURRY! H-HURRY!"

The garage door slammed shut.

"L-LEAVE THEM! H-HIDE!" Sylvia wailed

The pencil began to move slowly as Bernie wrote the first answer.

"Y-you're d-doing it!" Sylvia said in amazement. "Y-you're r-really d-doing it. Y-you m-must be m-magic!"

The front door banged open and she whimpered

"Number nine's a bit of an old prob-job," Bernie said slowly.

"LEAVE IT! LEAVE IT!" she urged her.

"We're ho-ome!" her mother called up.

"J-JUST LEAVE IT! P-PLEASE!"

Bernie liked maths. "Don't panic, you. I'm thinking," she drawled.

Heavy footsteps came trudging up the stairs.

"G-GO! R-RUN! H-HIDE! OH GOD! P-PLEASE!"

"Got it. Yeah – Got it," Bernie announced carefully writing "twenty-eight-point-five". Number ten's easy," she said. "Look. One of those ten-per-cent ones. I reckon you could do this. Look, Sylvie."

Sylvia screamed in terror. "NO! NO! MISS IT OUT!"

The door handle squeaked!.

"There," Bernie said, looking pleased and smoothing her hair back. "Finished."

"Qu-quick! In the w-wardrobe," Sylvia gasped, pulling open the big walnut doors.

"Okay, okay," Bernie said, still thinking about the maths. "Keep your hair on, you!"

Sylvia pushed her in – *hard* . . . The bedroom door opened behind her, making her yelp as if she'd been hit. "T-tidying it u-up!" she said in answer to a question they didn't ask. Her mother was quivering and waving a sheet of paper about.

"You'll never guess, Sylvia!" she said. "There's a race! A mile race! It's just *perfect* for you! The winner gets a *wish!* Can you believe that? A WISH! And it's for Year Sixers! *Now* we'll show them what you can do!"

Not more running! Please!

Her mother pulled Sylvia's shoes off. "We must start today!" she said. "Start working on one-mile runs. About three a day, I think. By Friday, you'll be at your peak."

Her father read the letter from The Queen, carefully. "We mustn't neglect her studies though, Christine," he said. "She's still got to fit her work in."

"Oh, don't worry about that!" her mother said. "Sylvia's

going to be world *champion* one day! And this Wishing Race will get her noticed, Walter." Chris Starr was always telling them about how she'd been picked for the 1980 Olympics but had been prevented from running because of her knee ligament trouble. *She* could have been a world champion.

"How did you get on with those percentages?" he asked her.

"Oh, s-simple," she said. She bit her lip as he bent to look at Bernie's work.

"The school race is on Friday," her mother gabbled excitedly. "You'll win that easily. Then there's an Area Final. Then a Regional Final. The National Final is at Buckingham Palace. That's when you get your wish!" She began unbuttoning Sylvia's shirt.

He was staring down at it hard. What if it's all wrong? All complete Rumble-split-skin? A little cry squeezed past her throat.

"What is it? What's wrong?" her mother asked anxiously.

"N-nothing."

The end of his red pen moved . . . then again . . . and again . . . He turned and looked at her. "Amazing!" he said. "A-level work at her age! And they're all correct!" She wanted him to *smile*. To be really *pleased* with her . . . But he still had his usual grumpy old face – even though he laughed to her mother. "I'll show these to Nigel on Monday," he said (Nigel Hanger was her class teacher). "I'll show him what she's capable of with some good old-fashioned discipline!"

"You can wear that new track-suit!" her mother said as if she was presenting her with the world's most wonderful gift. "New project – New thinking – New gear. It's very important to get your mind right, Sylvia. It's in the wardrobe, isn't it?"

"No, Mummy! It's okay!" But it was too late. Her mother had pulled the doors open and was flipping through the hangers . . . Then she saw it . . . Squeezed in at the far right-hand end. She tugged it out. "Come on!" she said. "One mile before lunch. Get this on and get downstairs, at the double!" She almost ran from the room, her husband right behind her, still complaining about that science that had got to be done.

Both wardrobe doors were swinging on their hinges but it looked very still and dark inside. "Where are you?" she whispered, biting her lip again.

Nothing!

"Ber-nie! Ber-nie! Where are you?"

"In Nar-nia . . . Nar-nia . . ." Bernie's ghost-voice answered. The clothes shook as she unrolled herself from the ball she'd curled into. "I'm triple-jointed!" she announced, springing out.

They clung on to each other, giggling.

"Syl-via! Hur-ry up!" her mother called.

"Come on!" Sylvia told Bernie. "Triple-joint yourself out of that window! TRIPLE QUICK!"

3

Sylvia

Friday 10th March

Sylvia ran and ran that week. She even ran through her sleep . . . But in her dreams she was always running away from something – Something she daren't turn round to look at.

On the Thursday her mother rested her.

On the Friday she had a special race breakfast. About a *ton* of thick brown bread for carbohydrates and energy.

In morning break she was shut in class as usual, by herself. She screwed up her *fourth* attempt at sketching a stupid map of Great Britain and threw it down. This time she would begin at Cornwall. She didn't hear the squeak of the classroom door . . . and she didn't see Bernie creeping up to her little alcove-cell. "YAH! BOO!" Bernie yelled in her ear!

All week she'd been keeping away from Bernie – terrified her father might see them together. But it was great to see her suddenly right there. "B-BERNIE B-BRAIN-BOX!" she sang out. They took hands and danced round. "You sh-shouldn't be in here!" she said, throwing a glance at the door.

Bernie laughed at her and patted her face. "And *you* shouldn't be so mega-frightened of them!" she said. "They can't *eat* you! . . WAH!" She pounced on Sylvia, pretending to gobble her up.

Sylvia squealed. "H-he could c-come in!"

"WELL? We could sing our little song for him, then, couldn't we?"

Sylvia grinned. "He'd have a *heart attack!*"

"Or a FART ATTACK!" Bernie shrieked into her face.

Sylvia gasped and slammed a hand over Bernie's mouth.

"You must *like* staying in." It was like Bernie was accusing her.

"NO I DON'T!" Sylvia was certain!

"Right, then!" Bernie grabbed her wrists. "You're coming out with us, you!"

"I c-can't! I C-CAN'T!" Sylvia protested, struggling and laughing.

"You'll be a MEGA-HIT!" Bernie said, dragging her and bashing the desks out of place. "Everyone wants to see the Lice Girls . . . *'If you wanna be my liver!'*" she sang . . . *"Starring starry-eyed Starr!"*

A crowd of kids had gathered at the window.

"N-NO! N-NO!" Sylvia complained, hooking an ankle round a table-leg.

Bernie let her go. "You mustn't let them bully you," she told her. "You're just a *puppet* they can do any old thing with, you!"

Sylvia laughed. "I know, I know," she said.

"Start being *yourself,*" Bernie said. "*NOW.* Start doing what *you* want to do. Like that dopey race after break. Don't run in it if you don't want to."

"I've *got* to."

"You *haven't!* Just *refuse.* They can't *make* you."

The classroom door banged open and Sylvia whimpered and fell back onto her chair.

The kids flew from the window.

The *shape* of her father – his actual *shape* – frightened

15

her. He came at her very slowly which was *really* dangerous – like a slow, heavy, wild rhino. His face twitched with anger and she cried out, cowering from him. "Ex-plain! Ex-plain!" he demanded standing over her.

Bernie slipped herself in between them and cheekily stared right into the beast's eyes . . . He WALLOPED her! Knocking her across Sylvia's desk. Sylvia screamed. But Bernie jumped straight up and looked right into the eyes of the Devil again. *And she sang to him!* In her beautiful, clear voice:

> *"If you wanna be her father –*
> *If you wanna be her Dad.*
> *Treat her like you love her!*
> *Like a father wou-ould."*

He knocked her flying again, right down onto the floor! But she got up *once more* and faced him.

"YOU GIP-SIES!" He spat the words out as if they tasted nasty. "LIARS! CHEATS! THIEVES! ALL OF YOU!"

Sylvia thought she was actually going to be *sick*. She felt so *faint!* "R-Run! R-Run!" she pleaded. How could she just stare at him like that?

"Don't *ever* speak to my daughter again, gipsy!" he ordered her. Then a horrible idea frightened him and he began to shake. "You two aren't *friends*, are you?" he asked.

"Oh n-no, Daddy!" she said taking her eyes away from Bernie's face.

"You don't actually *like* her, do you?"

"N-no Daddy," Sylvia said. "She's n-not my t-type, is she?" Sylvia, you traitor! You traitor!

"Hear that, gipsy girl?" he said. "That's it, exactly! You're not our *type!* Now get yourself to my office! AT ONCE! D'you hear?"

16

Bernie didn't seem to be in any hurry. She just shook her head at him.

Oh, Go! Go! Before he kills you!

"You're just a big bully!" she said calmly. "I'm going out to play." Walter Starr gasped and raised his arm to thump her again. *But she just stood there WAITING FOR IT!* Looking right into his face.

Sylvia heard him sort of sigh, then his hand fell limp and useless.

Bernie smiled at him, forcing him to look away. She had *won*. Then she simply turned and walked slowly out to play. In her own time . . . Sylvia looked down at the floor again, biting her lip.

* * *

She couldn't stop thinking about it. Someone had stood up to her father. It kept coming back into her head again and again. His raised hand. Bernie, absolutely still. That look on her face. His hand drops. She walks out.

Now they were on the school field for the race. Sylvia was in lane three, warming up. She shot a glance at Bernie sitting with Year Six. She looked sad. "DON'T RUN!" she mouthed. She shuffled her feet and crouched for a good push-off. Her mother signalled with a little bobbing movement and she crouched lower in response . . . Bernie saw this and stood, dancing like a puppet with floppy legs and arms . . . Sylvia quickly looked back at the track.

"ON YOUR MARKS!" her father commanded.

She fixed her eyes on the white tram-lines and started her breathing.

"GET SET!"

She began rocking. And gripping with her toes.

"GO!"

17

She lurched forward, sticking to her left-hand line.

"COUNT, DON'T LOOK!" She heard her mother's instructions. Yes. She must count. And concentrate on her rhythm. Forget the others.

She leaned into the bend and she heard her mother again: "One-two. One-two. One-two." Like a clock ticking out time for her.

When they broke out of their lanes, she slipped in behind the leader and sheltered in his slip-stream as she'd been taught.

Year Six were screaming and yelling like nutcases! Her mother stepped forward and tapped herself on the shoulder. "Oh no!" Sylvia told herself. "Too stiff! Too stiff!" She immediately let her shoulders drop to fully open her lungs. She just *had* to look at Bernie who was making a "You're just hopeless" face at her.

Last lap! Her throat was on fire! The boy in front was *good*!

Her father had run across to the back straight. She saw him glaring at her and she whimpered.

"FASTER! COME ON!" he boomed. *She couldn't!* She hurt all over! He shook his big fist. She looked into his eyes. *Daddy! Nice Daddy!* And she actually began to *sprint* for him, shooting herself forward . . . and into the lead.

She ran for the tape in her beautiful, perfect rhythm – her head rocking, her elbows jabbing. Like a new world champion!

And there they both were, at the finish. They looked different! Yes! They were smiling, surely! Waving at her! Their faces were full of love! Oh, yes! Yes! A new Mummy and Daddy!

She flew across the line and right up to them. At last! They were going to hug her, kiss her, swing her round! *Oh, all the torture doesn't matter! I forgive you . . !* Her mother turned away to write down her time. Her father began blustering and spitting. "You almost *lost* it!" he yelled at her. "What's up with you today, girl?"

But I won! I won! Oh, I won for you, Daddy!

* * *

Sylvia had eaten her *sensible,* MEGA-BORING, packed lunch by herself and was trying to make a bed with the hard classroom chairs. Behind her, the window creaked and the room was full of Bernie's singing: "*If you wanna be my larvae!*"

Sylvia laughed, ran over and stuffed some of her long hair into her mouth. "You're a *hero!*" she said.

"And YOU'RE the fastest puppet in the world!"

"I know, I know. But I *wish* I was as brave as you."

Bernie pulled Sylvia's sad mouth up into a smile. "Well you *could* be, Silver Sylvie, if you tried!" she said. "If you just *DID IT!*"

"No, no," Sylvia said, shaking her head. "I couldn't."

Bernie looked over at the chairs. "What are you doing, you?" she said.

"Making a bed, I'm whacked! And I'm supposed to be *thinking seriously* about my wish."

"Oh, brill!" Bernie said, pushing her hair back. "What are you going to wish for?"

"No idea! I expect they'll tell me."

"DON'T BE SUCH A PEANUT BRAIN! What do *you* want? For *yourself?*"

Sylvia looked shyly at her friend. "I just want them to like me," she said.

"HUH! The Queen ain't into MIRACLES! What else?"

"A new brain, I think!"

"Don't be so PATHETIC!" Suddenly Bernie grabbed hold of her through the window. "It's OBVIOUS!" she said "We must be as thick as custard!"

"Well I am, anyway,"

"No! Your wish! You've got to ask the Queen to make them leave you alone! To stop being *cruel* to you!"

Sylvia smiled and looked down at the tiles. "I don't think I could ask for that," she said.

"You *could!* You *could!*" Bernie insisted. "Give me that piece of paper." She stretched herself right in and wrote:

"I wish I didn't have to do that running with my mother. I wish I didn't have to do all that extra work with my father. I wish they'd stop bullying me. I wish I could have some freedom, like other kids. I wish I wasn't a PUPPET!

Sylvia stared at the lovely handwriting. "Maybe I *could,*" she said. "They wouldn't know. You put your wish in this special envelope. Nobody else sees it."

"Well do it, then *you!*"

"Could she? Really? Was it possible?" "I could come out with you whenever I wanted to, then!" she said.

"Like most people," Bernie informed her.

"And listen to your music!"

"And do the Lice Girls!"

"And watch telly!"

"As much as you like!"

"Coo-ee-ee! MEGA-BOOM-BANG! Watch telly whenever you like!" She hadn't seen Bernie's eyes slip away towards the classroom . . .

Her mother almost knocked her over as she barged past and slammed the window shut.

"AWAY WITH YOU!" Walter Starr shouted through the glass. But Bernie had beaten him once and she didn't move! Sylvia felt his powerful great hand gripping her arm and he dragged her across the classroom, bashing tables on the way and bruising her legs. "You are NOT to talk to that CREATURE again!" he fumed.

"N-no. I w-won't," she said. *I will ! I will!*

He put the trembling Wish Envelope down in front of her . . . and her mother carefully placed a shiny booklet beside it.

"W-what's that?" Sylvia asked.

"Broom Bank School for Gifted Children." Her mother's voice was all wobbly. "This is probably the best school in the country for young athletes, Sylvia!"

"*And* for high academic standards," her father added.

She stared at the ancient mansion on the cover. "*Broom Bank – A fast-track school for fast-track youngsters,*" she read.

"It's only twenty miles away," he told her, as if this was all that mattered. "It's residential, of course, but we could come and see you whenever we wished – Help you with your homework."

"And your running."

"It's a wonderful school, Sylvia," he told her. "Real, old-fashioned discipline and hard work. They deliberately put you under pressure to get the best out of you."

"I'M NOT GOING! I'M NOT GOING!" She could almost feel the dark building closing around her.

"It's a very hard school to get into, isn't it Walter?"

"Oh yes. They're very fussy about who they have at Broom Bank – lucky things – they can pick and choose. You couldn't just walk into Broom Bank – they're full at the moment anyway – unless . . ." He took the dark blue Wishing Card from its envelope.

"Unless it was my wish," she said for him.

"*Exactly! Exactly!*" He smoothed out the Wishing Card

and handed her a new Berol handwriting pen that was cold and smelt of the stock cupboard. "Best handwriting," he said. "Here you are. We've written down what to put."

She read his scribbled notes: *"If I win the Wishing Race Final I would wish to go to Broom Bank School for Gifted Children in the West Midlands. I'd like to stay there until I pass my exams for Cambridge University."*

Bernie was staring at her from the window. She couldn't escape those eyes . . . she leaned forward over the Wishing Card and wrote her wish . . . slid it into the royal envelope . . . and stuck it down. Without anyone seeing.

4

Isaac

Wednesday 8th March

Isaac knew he was going to die. This was his fourth attack since Sunday. The fourth! And they were getting worse . . . sort of dangerous . . . and frightening . . . These were the ones that old doctor had told him about.

A red-hot electric pain whooshed down his left leg and jerked him across the couch. "Git away! Git away!" he hissed into the chattering of *Neighbours*.

His Ma was squashed up in the window-bay, ironing and dreaming. She hadn't seen. He never ever let her see his pain.

Another hot bolt shook his small body and he thumped the flea-bag cushion beside him. He had to get away. Up to his room. Where he could turn his reggae music up real loud and yell out and no-one would hear.

She was smiling and nodding. Talking to her folks back home in her head.

He gripped his tubular-steel crutches, his Number Sevens, and wriggled his bum forwards. Isaac had been two years old when he'd had his Number Ones.

"Now!" he mumbled and hauled himself up onto his feet.

"Isaac!" she said, eyeing him suspiciously. "You all right, boy?"

"Yeah. I'm okay, Ma", he said. "I'm jus' goin' upstairs."

She narrowed her eyes and studied him more closely . . . but he had this new trick ready. Long John Silver. He bent right over, screwed his face up and croaked: "Ah gotta go now shipmates." He began hobbling towards the stair door. "Up aloft. me lads!" Then he twisted himself back towards her and sort of cackled his new song:

"Long John Silver
Had a parrot that was sicky.
Now he's Long John Yellow,
Green and sticky!"

His mother whooped, her laughter lighting the room with a flash of Caribbean sunshine. He'd done it! He'd fooled her. He lifted the latch and slipped out.

"You go careful, now, Mr Silver!" he heard her calling as he bumped up the stairs. "You mind there ain't no cut-throats hidin' up there!"

He sort of rolled into his room. And stabbed his CD into life, Bob Marley instantly booming a thumping beat through the house. He tumbled onto his bed, squirming with pain. "Ah! Get off! Get off, you poo-face!" he screamed at it.

Isaac was small for his age, with a round, dark face. But inside, he was big and strong. Here it comes again! He pulled at his useless leg and tried to roll over. He'd found out that if he dodged away, just as the pain came, it sort of missed him. But he wasn't quick enough.

Pow! It got him. *Zap!* Down his right side. "Gas-bum! Ye-ow! Ye-ow!" he yelled. It was a big one. Like molten lava erupting inside him. "Ahhh!" It hammered his right leg out straight with a huge, new force. *Wham!* Right into his pine cabinet! One of the drawers flew out and crashed to the floor in a heap of *Dennis the Menace* socks and West Ham underpants.

Somewhere, far far way, a door opened . . . He clenched a fist. Punched Bob Marley off. Bit his lip. And listened . . . His Ma was shuffling and squeezing herself into the tiny space at the bottom of the stairs . . .

"EYE-SUCK!" she called up. "You okay, son?"

"Yeah, I'm fine, Ma," he told her.

"You not havin' one of them ol' attacks, are you Issy?"

He laughed his "Don't be daft!" laugh. "I've told y', Ma. I ain't had one of them since afore Christmas," he said. "I'm really gettin' better, Ma. Jesus' truth I am."

"Well hell-e-lu-yah!" she said. "When it comes t' miracles, the Good Lord can show those know-it-all doctors a thing or two!"

She was still there . . . listening . . . balanced between truth and hope . . . Then the shuffling again . . . and she was gone.

The attack was over. Isaac sighed a massive sigh and laid back . . . Sweating . . . worn out . . . and sort of peaceful.

* * *

At 2am, in the deepest dark of the night, the switch on the landing clicked right down into Isaac's dreams, as it did every night. He opened his eyes and saw the large outline of his Ma in the doorway.

"Come on now, son," she said gently. "Time for me t' bash y' about." She chuckled and coughed.

Isaac dreamily pushed at his quilt and rolled over onto his tummy, ready for the heavy massage that helped his leg muscles and his circulation.

She would do it again before breakfast.

Then at lunchtime in the school office.

And every day after school.

And at bed-time.

Day after day. Year after year.

He felt the large, warm hands beginning to pummel his calf muscles.

He wished and wished and wished she didn't have to do this. It was wearing her out. She looked so ill these days. And *Why! Why! Why!* did she have to work so hard? At that warehouse?

"That's great, Ma," he muttered sleepily. When she began coughing, his eyes flicked wide open. "No! Please! No!" She wasn't going to . . .

Then a bigger one and he felt her hands fly up off his legs. He rolled over onto his back. And the whole bed began to shake as the rough coughs threw her about. He couldn't help her. He just stared into her wet face.

"Ah'm okay, son. Ah'm jes' fine," she gasped.

"It's that rain, Ma. An' the cold. England's a-killin' y', Ma!" He watched, helpless, as she bent over double, trying to sort of bite the air for breath. Then he had an idea and called out: *"Jamaica, Ma! Jamaica! Silvery sunshine, Ma! White sand! Granpa George! Heat!"*

Something in her throat crackled and seemed to break and she sucked in a long, sweet breath.

"Tell me about Granpa George, Ma. Tell me about when you were a girl. How y' helped him build that ol' boat-house."

She wiped her eyes and snuggled up real close. "Ah should think you know more about that ol' hut than ah do, Issy. Yeah, it was a fine place all right. Me an' m' daddy, why we jes' built it there, right on top of its own little jetty. Ah used t' sit 'n' drop shells through the floor jes t' hear 'm splash in the ocean below."

He loved it when she talked like this. That look on her face. Like she was a girl again.

"The sand was so white, Issy. An' the air so hot. Why – Y' felt jes' like y' could suck in the light with y' breath."

She was breathing real slow now. Real easy. Like the air was suddenly filling her with life.

"Ah do swear, son, that water was so clear you could jes' dip y' hands right in an' lift those pretty little fish right into y' basket . . ."

When she got up to go he sat up straight and said "I'm gonna take you back there, Ma. Yessir! I am!"

"Sure you are, boy." she said, laughing and shuffling out.

Isaac stared into his own darkness. "One day," he said aloud. "One day . . . jes' you see!"

5

Isaac

Thursday 9th March

"Somethin's happenin'," Isaac told his mates as they dragged in for assembly. "Somethin's going on, innit?"

"Yeah. Look at Buttercup," Mishah said. "She's like a flea with the hiccups!"

"She's had a letter from the Queen, right?" Bon told them, scratching his bum and treading on some Year Five fingers. "That's what everyone says, right?"

"P'raps she'll forget about nickin' me at break then!" Mishah hoped.

Isaac hated it when Mishah got seriously in trouble. Which was nearly every day! She couldn't stop pinching things or smashing things to bits.

"SIT, BOY!" she ordered him roughly. But she placed the chair behind him with great care and held people away protectively while he settled himself. She sat on the floor beside him and made hate faces at people as they came in. Mishah hated ever single, yuck-faced person in the world! Except Isaac.

He was so glad to sit down. He started wriggling on his ___ praying he wouldn't get an attack in assembly. ___ e bashed their elbow into the side of his face. ___ or-ry-ry!" Satchi sang out, smoothing his slicked-back hair and grinning. "I must have tripped, Your Lordship." He really hated Isaac having this special place to sit.

Mishah saw it and quickly back-butted her head into Satchi's stomach, winding him. "Sit down, oil-slick!" she said.

"Shush now, everybody!" Mrs Buttercup called out. "I've something very important to tell you." Isaac smiled at her. She was just a crazy girl, really. Pretending to be a Head. "This morning everybody, all of us – *all of us!* – have had a letter from BUCKINGHAM PALACE!" She jumped as if the words had bitten her and Isaac smiled again.

"And why should the Queen write to us hands up?" she asked them.

"'Spect she wants that Lunch-time Supervisor job!" Satchi sneered.

"She wants us all to *get fit!*" she said, hopping a little.

"Oh no!" Bon moaned. "I hate getting fit, right?"

"You just like getting *fat!* You porky!" Satchi sniggered.

"Her Majesty says we are the most unfit children ever to live in this Kingdom!" she went on. "She says we have all been neglecting our bodies have we-ee-ee?" she asked swooping low over the infants. "We've all been stuffing our hungry little faces in front of the telly have we-ee-ee?"

Mishah looked up at Isaac angrily. Fancy old Buttercup going on about healthy bodies when *he* was sitting there. "What about *her* body then?" she said to him. "She's about as tough as Snow White, she is!"

But Isaac didn't mind being different. Nearly everyone in school was really great to him.

Mrs Buttercup's voice fell into a story-telling tone. "Now," she said. "The Queen has written to us today – and to *all* Primary Schools – to tell us . . . to prepare for . . . THE WISHING RACE!"

"I could win that, right?" Bon said. "I could be a World

Champion wisher, I could, right?" Isaac laughed and prodded Bon's soft tummy with a Number Seven.

"The Wishing Race is a *running* race," she went on. She looked up towards the back of the hall. "For our Year Sixers." Year Five moaned out loud. "The Queen has commanded us to find our fastest Year Six runner."

Satchi was looking around at them, threatening everyone with his eyes. "It's me, innit?" he said to them. He shot his hand up and yelled, "ME MISS!"

Isaac was glad Mrs Buttercup gave him a mean look. "Our fastest *runner,* Satchi. Not our fastest *drugs-runner!*" Isaac could see she was sorry she'd said that and she hurried on. "*Whoever* our best runner is," she said, "will have to race against other schools – schools around us, in Docklands."

Isaac had never heard it so quiet.

"If they *win,*" she explained, her eyes wide, "well . . . then they run in the *City Race* . . . against Year Sixers from all over London!" She skipped a little dance of excitement.

"If they win the *London* race!" she told them, "they go in the *South of England* race!" It was like she was telling them there really *were* fairies at the bottom of the playground!

"Now!" she said, her voice cooing. "Now we come to the *wonderful* bit . . . The winner of the South of England race goes to THE PALACE! . . ." She stumbled backwards as if shocked by the words. "To run in THE WISHING RACE! . . ." She swept low over the infants again. "Against children from *all over the entire country! . . .*" Her arms zoomed out to show how big the country was. "*In front of television cameras!* AND THE QUEEN!" She curtsied low as if the Queen was standing there in their school hall.

"Why's it called The Wishing Race, Miss?" Bon called out.

She whispered her secret. "Because the winner gets a wish, Bon. From the Queen. Any wish they want."

"Could you wish for a motor-bike, Miss?" Bon asked.

"You can't even stay on a normal bike, you can't!" Satchi sneered.

Mishah was interested now. "What about your Mum and Dad getting together again, Miss? Could you have that?"

"What about playing for Arsenal?" Satchi asked. "Yeah. Be a striker for Arsenal!"

"What about a horse, Miss?"

"Or a trip to Disney World?"

"For a whole year!"

"A swimming pool!"

Isaac knew what *he'd* wish for. A lovely, long trip to Jamaica for his Ma. To see her father, Gran'pa George. And the sunshine. To make her better again. "Hey! Ma! I've won this Wishing Race!" her fantasised. "I'm taking you to Jamaica, Ma! Like I promised!" He smiled at his dream.

They were going to have their own race to find the fastest Year Sixer and Mrs Buttercup was collecting names. "It'll be tomorrow. After assembly," she told them. "Up at Dockside Gardens. We'll all go along to watch. Now then, anyone else?"

Bon took ages to untangle his legs and stand up with the other runners.

"*You*, Bon?" she asked.

"Might as well have a go," he said. Everyone laughed.

"Seven then. Seven runners in our own little Wishing Race. Now! Last chance. Are there any more?"

"Don't be stupid!" Isaac told himself. "You can't run! Blimey – You can only just WALK!" . . . The attack came at him so suddenly. Like a lightning bolt. Zig-zagging down his right leg. Rocketing it out straight. *Wham!* into the chair in front.

Mrs Story-Cookson felt the chair go from under her.

"Ooh! Ooh!" she cried. And she fell sideways right on top of little Rosie Brown, completely squashing her with her huge boobs!

Wow! What power!

"ISAAC!" she yelled.

He could have kicked a football a *mile!*

"Look at my frock!"

He could have leapt over a *house!*

"And poor, poor Rosie. *Isaac* – Look at Rosie!"

"Sorry, Miss." He was struggling to stand. "I was just . . ."

Mishah was goggle-eyed. What was the dung-brain trying to do?

"I was just . . . just . . . just . . . trying to stand up," he said. There. He was up. He looked right into Mrs Buttercup's wondering face. "Eight now, Miss," he said.

She looked at him as though he'd just popped out of a conjuror's hat. "Oh, Isaac!" she trilled. "Are you going to . . .?"

"Yes, Miss."

"I mean – can you?"

"Yes, Miss. I can, Well I *think* I can."

"Oh Isaac. That's truly wonderful."

"I've got a plan, Miss."

Satchi looked disgusted. "Crutches and things aren't allowed!" he complained. "It ain't fair. He can't run anyway! He never runs!"

Mishah knew how to shut him up. She grabbed both legs of his track-suit bottoms and yanked hard, *downwards.* The whole school roared and Satchi tried to cover himself up. "NO PANTS! NO PANTS! NO PANTS!" they chanted.

6

Isaac

Friday 10th March

The whole school had trooped up to Dockside Gardens and the race was about to begin.

"I'm gonna sick up!" Isaac said.

"Well sick up over Buttercup then!" Mishah told him.

Isaac was leaning on his Number Sevens so that she could roll up his track-suit bottoms. They were huge and red and old. Like baggy bloomers. Mishah had found them in lost property for him.

"You look like Father flippin' Christmas!" Satchi scoffed.

"Come on, runners! Make a line! Level with me!" Mr Burton called, raising his arm.

"Oh no!" Isaac moaned.

"You don't have to do it, do you?" Mishah said. "You can come over with us and watch."

Isaac followed her with his eyes as she walked over towards everyone standing in front of *The Wheelhouse* restaurant.

What a poo-brain I am! What a twit-headed poo-brain! Standing out here in front of the school. For a *running race!* What a gonk!

Mrs Buttercup smiled at him.

I could say I feel ill – Well, I do! Then go and stand with the others.

"It's round the boat-shed," Mr. Burton instructed them. "Then over to the life-buoy, okay?" Isaac noticed a white cargo-ship edging past them on the grey River Thames. "Round the flag-pole. And then follow the path back here. Three laps. Got it?"

He turned and looked at Mishah. "What shall I do?" he shrugged.

"On your marks!"

"Oh, this is daft!" he told himself and began limping away.

"Get set!"

"I feel sick, Miss!" he called out.

"Go!"

The whole school rose up in front of him, yelling and screaming. All eyes on the seven runners behind him. He felt stranded and alone.

* * *

During her coffee-break, leaning against her fork-lift truck, Isaac's Ma was listening to her mate who'd been to the school. When she heard about the race she took the Mars Bar out of her mouth. And when she heard that *Isaac* was in it she *screamed* . . . dropped her mug . . . and hurried out of the warehouse, half-running, half-waddling.

* * *

Isaac began limping over towards Mishah. But someone sort of shuffling down the steps and waving at him frantically made him stop dead! It couldn't be! It was! His Ma!

"ISSY! ISSY-BOY!" she gasped. "What you *doin,'* you

crazy, boy?" She was hanging onto Mrs Buttercup for support. Her face looked yellow and sick.

Jamaica! he remembered and turned to see how far they'd got. They were leaning over to go round the boat-shed . . .

His plan was all to do with that Science lesson, when they'd worked on springs. Mishah and the others stared at him in amazement. He was sort of crouching down low like a frog – His Number Sevens spread wide like wings . . . "You have to compress your spring – Push it down really hard," he remembered.

"ISSY! ISSY!" he heard his Ma yelling. "Yo' come right back here, now. D' y' hear?"

"He's crazy!" Mishah said.

Isaac was very still . . . waiting . . .

"ISSY!"

The pain rose like a wave and he screwed his face up against it.

"YOU GIT RIGHT BACK HERE T' ME! YO' NAUGHTY BOY!"

He gripped his Number Sevens ready for take-off. 'This is a stupid idea! I knew it wouldn't work!'

Everyone heard him yell out as the wave of pain crashed down inside his right leg. "YE-OW-OW!"

"Mah poor boy!"

He felt his leg shoot out straight . . . and he shot up like a Jack-in-the-Box!

"Lordy! He's a flyin'!"

When he landed, he crouched low on his left foot for a moment. "YE-OW-OW!"

"ISSY! ISSY!"

He felt himself jerked up in the air again . . . and down on his right foot.

Mishah's eyes were bulging.

"YE-OWCH!" Into the air, left. "YE-OWCH!" Into the air, right.

Isaac found he could control it. He had to sort of tense himself inside to stop and start the pains. He began moving forwards with a rhythm.

"HE CAN RUN! HE CAN RUN!" the kids yelled.

"Lordy-be! Lordy-be!" his mother moaned, collapsing onto a seat.

"I can run! I can run! YE-OWCH! I can run!" It was the greatest feeling in the world. The others were behind the boat-shed. He'd never catch them but it didn't matter. He was running! For the first time in his life.

"Look at him go!" Mr Burton called out. "He's like a whirring octopus!"

The deadly power of Isaac's illness shot him forward. Faster and faster.

"He's catching them up, you know!" Mr. Burton said.

He couldn't slow down. It was like he was being thrown along. "Oh no! Oh no!" he pleaded, trying not to tumble over between his clattering Number Sevens.

"He's nearly caught them!"

He thought he was going to faint with the pain. He *zoomed* past Bon. "See y', right?" Bon called to him.

The yells of the school blasted him.

His Ma was wagging a finger at him.

Mrs Buttercup was wiping her eyes.

Mishah had a strange look on her face.

They heard him screaming as he rattled past them.

"Only Satchi now! Only Satchi!" he gasped. Satchi turned back to him. Grinning an evil grin. "Come on then, Peg-a-leg!" he scoffed. "You look like a flippin' windmill on legs!" But he was amazed to see Isaac there. And a bit frightened. He clenched his fists and forced himself to go faster.

"Oh, Satchi's got him. Satchi's gonna win it," Mr Burton said.

When Isaac saw his Ma he nearly stumbled. She had flopped back on her seat. Her face was all grey. And she could hardly breathe. "Oh no!" he said realising. "Don't say *she's* gonna die too! Don't say she's bin cheatin' *me!*"

Mishah's eyes were fixed hard on the crazy little gonk! She heard him yell "Jamaica! Ye-owch! Jamaica! Ye-owch!"

Isaac's armpits had been rubbed raw on his crutches but he swore and pushed even harder. And he sort of gripped himself inside and let the big pains come. And the huge, jaguar leaps!

"Jesus be praised!" his Ma said, forcing herself to sit up.

Mishah clenched her fists and hissed "Come on! Come on!"

Mrs Buttercup couldn't believe her eyes and was smiling her "Walt-Disney-film" smile.

He was level with Satchi. Everyone was yelling and hopping about like mad fleas!

"Get back YOU FREAK! Get back!" Satchi sneered.

There was Mr Burton holding the tape. One more last effort. "Aah! Aah! Aah!" he screamed.

"Yes! Yes!" Mishah yelled.

"Isaac wins! Isaac wins!" Mr Burton announced.

Mishah ran over and hugged him and she felt him go limp and slip down between her arms.

The sky looked wrong. Sort of extra bright. Silvery. Then his Ma appeared, nodding and laughing. "Mah boy! He ken run! Jesus is a-mendin' his body, folks. YO' BAD BOY! YO' BAD BOY!" she scolded.

Isaac felt he was drifting into a lovely, sleepy peace . . .

Mishah stared at him in horror. "GET BACK! GET BACK! Give him some air!" she cried.

The world began to wobble and swim . . . then went black.

Satchi stood over him like a victor. "If he's dead *I* win!" he said. "*I* was second!"

Mishah thumped his stomach so hard he gasped and farted at the same time.

"Mah boy ain't a dyin'!" his Ma said, bending and stroking his warm face. "He's a-gettin' better I tell y'!" She looked up at the sky, smiling at Jesus and coughing.

7

Hazel

Saturday 1st January

Hazel's father was leaving them. "Don't go," she muttered against the kitchen window. She wiped her breath-mist off the glass. There he was again. Another box of clothes – Plonk! Into the back of the Volvo. He saw her watching and looked away. "Please, Father-man," she whispered.

Computer now. Just dumped in any old how! Usually, he was so fussy. She saw the backgammon box slide off and empty itself. They'd only been playing it on Sunday! The row they'd made! Screaming! Yelling! Tears of laughter streaming down her face . . ! "World Champ, five! Hazelnut four!" he'd announced at the end. If only it could be Sunday again!

The car rocked when he jumped in and Hazel moaned. The headlights lit the fresh snow up so brightly it made her blink. The engine struggled against the bitter cold. She jumped   down . . . Barged past the big wooden table . . . Leap-frogged over her mother who was scrubbing the back hall floor and pretending all this wasn't happening . . . and charged out to the farmyard.

The big car was slowly crunching away from her, dragging two shiny scars across the smooth cheek of snow. "Come back," she said very softly . . . watching as the red tail-lights went twisting down the track . . . over the beck bridge at the bottom . . . out along the road . . . into the lights of the village . . . and away.

Hazel shivered. To her left, across the High Peak valley, she could see the black outline of Claire's house on the moonlit, snowy hillside. "He's gone," she called out hopelessly to her friend.

In about one second flat she would have collapsed onto the snow, rolling around and howling up at the stars. But Father-man's words came back to her. "You must *control* your feelings, Hazel. You must be *master* of them or you'll be a *slave* to them."

She wiped the tears away as if he was watching, stamped hard and clenched her fists. "Right! Come on, Hazel!" she told herself as *he* told her every day. "The dogs have got to be doggied, my girl!"

That got her moving. Sort of ski-walking. And slithering. Over the cobbled farmyard. Towards Big Barn. Where he had shut the dogs in, away from the painful ice-air of the hill country.

Inside the barn, the warmth made her face tingle. And she sniffed the lovely, sweet smell of hay and dogs. She stood for a long moment with her eyes tight shut . . . Then she moved herself forward again. "Dogs-to-be-doggied. Dogs-to-be-doggied!" she told herself.

She had to laugh at them. The four, lean, brown-black fell-runners were as still as statues. Watching. Waiting for him. Greedy, with both paws up on the rusty fridge, was panting hungrily. Little Sneezy was being stupid – on his back, his muzzle twitching for a game. Sleepy was almost buried in straw and dozing, about one centimetre from the heater! And Doc was standing to attention. Alert. Guarding the others. *"He's not coming!"* she yelled at them. *"I'm gonna do it! Alright?"*

But *could* she? She'd helped him every night since she was about two. But he'd never let her actually DO IT. "Dogs-to-be-doggied. Dogs-to-be-doggied," she said. "Now . . . first of all . . . food." She pushed back the lid of the bran bin . . . But they'd heard something. Even Sleepy was up on his paws. Ears pricked. Muzzle sniffing the air.

She looked back at the door. The iron latch rattled. It swung open. And in came a walking snow-girl! *"Claire! You nut-case!"* Hazel roared.

Claire opened her arms wide to show off her whiteness and started singing:

> *"Dashing through the snow,"*
> *On a one-horse, open sleigh!"*

"Fancy trudging over here in *this* weather! You *idiot!*" Hazel scolded.

"Had to," she said with a grin. "Wanted to come over and thump you!" But she didn't finish her little speech. Even *she* couldn't say: "So you'd forget everything, You know. Your dad and things." She just threw her snowball at Hazel and shook her snow over Sneezy who jumped up, trying to bite it. "You mutt-head!" she said, rolling him over with her foot.

Hazel laughed at them. She was so glad Claire had come. But she didn't understand why this little bit of kindness made her cry. She blew her nose hard. "Don't you get them all stirred up!" she scolded. "We got all Dad's jobs to do." She pushed the biggest scoop into Claire's hand. "Here," she said. "Five lots of granules into the mixer."

"Yes Sir!" Claire said, saluting.

He'd got this secret winter-feed mix. High protein. High energy. She knew it off by heart. They were going to start *winning* some races this year – not just *running* them.

They fed them.

They weighed them.

Felt all over their warm, sleek bodies for injuries.

Brushed them hard.

And finally, Hazel recorded it all in his super-neat "Dog Book". In her very, very best handwriting . . . She couldn't believe she was actually writing in it.

Claire had made a sort of a crown out of straw. Well, she said it was a crown. Hazel thought it looked more like a crumpled tea-cosy! She stood very still while Claire perched it on her head. "I hereby declare," she announced, "that Hazel Elizabeth Fox is crowned Queen of the Doggy-Doos!" The crown slid off and the four dogs fought for it, yelping and snapping around their ankles. They looked good. She really had doggied the dogs.

* * *

They had this thing. Whenever they left each other they'd call out numbers till they couldn't hear them anymore. The next day they'd argue about who had shouted the last number.

Claire had slithered unsteadily across Little Paddock and disappeared into the whirling snowflakes. "TEN!" she hollered.

Hazel was sheltering behind Broken Shed. "E-LEV-EN!" she boomed.

"TWELVE!"

"THIR-TEEN!"

Claire must have been about at the bottom of the valley when Hazel heard a tiny, muffled "Fifty-two!"

"FIF-TY-THREE-EE!" she screamed into the thick snow-curtain and hurt her throat.

* * *

Back indoors, Hazel found her mother sweeping the brick floor of the kitchen *again*. When her wonderful Jeff had left her that afternoon – for no reason that *she* could understand – Pippy Fox had begun polishing and scrubbing and scurrying around like Mrs Tiggywinkle! As if she was trying to rub his actual image off the house . . . his very tall, jet-black haired, *lovely* image.

She didn't know Hazel was watching her. She looked so tiny – so helpless. Hazel felt so sorry for her. She had to blink a lot to stop herself crying. She was singing! Actually *singing*!

"*Brush-brush, brush-brush,*
Brush-brush, brush-brush
ALL the day.
Sweep those dirty marks
And all your CARES away,"

she squeaked, bashing the ancient floor with the broom.

"Doggied the dogs, Mum," Hazel told her.

She stopped and stared at Hazel with a face that looked a little wild and mad. "But he'll be back, you know. Oh yes. Jeffrey-man will be back!" she said.

Hazel took the broom out of her lifeless hands. She was taller than her mother – she was the tallest child in Year Six – and she looked down at the unhappy, tear-stained face. She tried to joke: "Oh, Cinderella!" she said. "You'll never go to the ball looking like that!"

There was a glimmer of a smile and her mother tried to joke back. "Oh, Fairy Godmother," she said. "They are so cruel to me here. Oh *why* did he go?" she bawled.

Hazel grabbed her and hugged her tight. She would always remember his explanation, sitting on the edge of her bed. "He wants a new life, Mum," she said. "He doesn't *want* to leave us but he has to."

"But WHY?"

"He's starting that new travel business thing in Manchester," she told her. "You know. 'Holidales'."

"But *why* must he do it without *us?*"

Hazel didn't know. She'd asked herself the same question all day. "Come on, Mum," she said, guiding her out of the kitchen. "Come and sit by the fire. I'll make you a coffee."

8

Hazel

Saturday 4th March

"Nine weeks exactly," Hazel said, chopping through the parsnip.

"And you haven't heard *one single thing* from him?" Claire asked her.

"No . . . well . . . no. Not really." There had just been that one brown envelope with a little cheque inside. She remembered smelling it. Kissing it. Rubbing it over her cheek. She hurried on and scraped the parsnip off the board and into the bowl.

Claire held her nose. "That looks ab-so-lute-ly dis-gust-ing!" she said.

"It's veggie stew."

"It looks like *hard sick!*"

"It's cheap," Hazel explained. "And it's the only thing I can get her to eat."

Claire put on her witch's voice. "You must EAT! EAT! EAT! Do you hear? Your finger still feels like a stick!"

Hazel picked up a pen and jotted a few more things on her shopping list. Claire grabbed the chopping knife and pretended to be cutting ropes from around Hazel. "Free the slaves! Free the slaves!" she chanted. Hazel looked down from her high stool and smiled at her. "I don't mind doing the jobs," she said.

"You liar!" Claire boomed.

"I like doing the dogs."

"You *hate* the cleaning!"

"I don't mind the cooking."

"You *loathe* the money. And the bills. And all that!"

Hazel's mother ran in and skipped round them like a small child. Then she snatched a saucepan from the drainer, squeezed it over her head and marched out singing:

> *"Oh, soldier, soldier,*
> *Won't you marry me*
> *With your musket, fife and drum?"*

"She's finally gone totally, absolutely doggy-doo-dah!" Claire said.

Hazel stared after her mother and called anxiously. "Have a little rest, Mum. Have a little rest." She strained to hear what she was doing out there. "She hasn't been to work for two weeks!" she muttered.

"That insurance office must be quiet without her!" Claire said. "All of *Sheffield* must be quiet without her!"

Hazel hadn't heard her. She was too full of worry. "They told her to take some time off. To get herself better," she said.

Claire saw the anxiety on her face. "Stop worrying, Haze," she said. "Come on. Let's go and do the dog-run."

Hazel laughed for the first time that day. "Yeah! Dog-run!" she said. "I'll finish this later!"

* * *

She loved the dog-run. She loved the feeling of running free over the fells. Four miles of panting up hills and slithering down slopes. Forcing the dogs into better and better times . . . Once more, she imagined herself running up to her father with the silver cup – "Best Pack in the Dale, Father-man!" she beamed.

When she was three he had carried her round.

When she was six, she'd run the whole way.

Last year she'd wanted to run ahead of them.

Now, on her own, she could go as fast as she liked.

Claire pressed the stop-watch, threw back the gate and let the stream of brown-black fur pour out of Little Pen. "Go for the record, Haze!" she called after them. "Go for twenty minutes!"

Hazel felt so full of energy today. The air was so fresh and clear. She could see all the tops as far as Saddle-back Mountain. She felt like a giant – as if she could just step right over them. "Twenty?" she thought. "I could do nineteen today. Or *anything*!"

Broken stile. One minute, twenty-seven seconds. The dogs were bobbing and bouncing ahead of her. Doc, yapping at them. Nipping them. Hazel was leaning right forward against the slope, her thick legs springing her up the spongy turf.

Sheep field. Two minutes, thirty. Good. Sleepy looked back for some sympathy. "Go! Go!" she shouted between breaths.

Summit-stone. Five, forty-two. Great. She looked down for a moment at the model cars winding their way through the valley far below. It always made her dizzy.

Down through Top Field. Six, nineteen.

Claire's house. Eight, forty-one. She turned and yelled back at them. Sneezy was in the lead. Look at him. He'd tucked himself in, real thin. He wasn't mucking about now. He was running as seriously as she was.

The bottom. Eleven, nineteen. Hecky-thump!

Over the beck. Scramble up the bank. Turn right, into the road. Right again, onto their track. The letter-box. She snatched a white envelope without stopping. Thirteen, thirty! *Thirteen, thirty!* She shook her watch.

Big Barn. Seventeen, fourteen.

* * *

Claire almost fell off the stone wall! "Gordon Bennett's Great Aunt Edna!" she exclaimed. "Seventeen, thirty! Seventeen, thirty-one! Thirty-two! Thirty-three! Thirty-four! Thirty-five! Thirty-six!"

Hazel crashed against the gate, Sneezy right behind her.

"SEVENTEEN MINUTES, THIRTY-SEVEN SECONDS!" Claire announced to the sheep over on the hillside. "An all-time, all-world, *all-universe* record!"

Hazel had slumped down against the gate-post, her head between her knees. Sneezy licking her face and panting warm dog-breath on her.

Claire tucked the blanket around her . . . and she put the little jackets they'd made over the dogs . . . and poured their warm milk and honey onto the soggy biscuits.

"I could get them down to sixteen before the races start," Hazel gasped. "They'll win everything – at least, Sneezy will!" She rubbed his head. Then her fingers found the envelope and began pulling at its edges. It had a Sheffield postmark and was addressed to her mother. But Hazel was in charge of everything these days. *"Dear Mrs Fox,"* she read. *"It is with great reluctance that I have to inform you* . . . Oh no!" she moaned.

"What?" Claire said. "What? Don't tell me. You *haven't* been chosen as the sexiest girl in Yorkshire!"

"Mum's lost her job," Hazel mumbled, staring up at the bright sky.

"Well, I wonder where it could be?" Claire joked, pretending to search.

"Don't be so stupid!" Hazel yelled at her. She'd *never* yelled at Claire before. *It's serious! Serious!"* Her head fell down between her knees again and her voice went very quiet. "There's already a pile of bills I can't pay. And there's no money left for shopping."

The hills had become silent. They could hear sheep in the distance and the lapping of the dogs' tongues in their bowls. And the revving of an engine as a car struggled up the track.

"CAR!" they said together and began scrambling down towards the house.

A fantastic cream car was nosing into the farmyard. It looked daft there. Like a really fancy present floating gently on MUD! "Heck!" Claire said. "Must be Her Royal Slyness! Or the Slime Sinister!"

A door flashed open and a fat man in a suit struggled out. "Look at that!" Claire joked. "A walrus driving a car!"

The other door opened and a really tubby boy sort of wobbled and flopped out. "PODGERS!" they both yelled. Archibald Rogers, their big enemy at school, stood there. Glaring at them. With his usual piggy-faced hatred.

Daddy Rogers cleared his throat. "Eh-hem. Allow me to introduce myself, young ladies. I'm Samuel Rogers," he said with a greasy grin that Hazel supposed was meant to be a smile. "I'm your mother's bank manager," he announced as though it was really good news. "I know all about the family's financial difficulties," he told them joyfully. "And about all the other . . . er . . . little problems." He winked at Hazel.

How did he? It was none of his business!

"But there's no need for you to worry yourself anymore, young lassie," he said. "Uncle Samuel has the answer to all your worries."

She hated him. *Hated* him.

"I've had this idea!" he said. "It's brilliant!" He obviously expected her to be impressed. *"We're going to buy your house!"*

"WHAT?" she yelled.

"Lots of lovely money for you! No more worries!"

"You are not!" she told him.

"If Archibald likes it, of course."

"NO!" she screamed. "NO! NO! NO!"

Archibald was trembling with excitement. Most people would jump up and down but the best *he* could do was to just tremble, like a jelly. "Want the dogs, Dad!" he insisted. "And the ducks! And the pond!"

"Why don't you jump *into* it? FROG-BOY!" Claire sneered.

"Want the *whole* house!" he demanded.

"YOU'RE NOT HAVING ANYTHING!" Hazel screamed. "IT'S *OUR* HOUSE! AND THEY'RE *OUR* DOGS!"

Samuel Rogers knew when it was time to make a gentle suggestion. "I think, perhaps, we ought to see what your good mother has to say, my dear," he said.

* * *

Pippy Fox came hurtling down the front stairs at about a hundred miles an hour. Hazel just about managed to catch her and stay on her feet. "Now Mum," she told her. "Concentration. Concentration."

"No! No, Dear! I haven't. The *Allbran* makes me go. Every morning."

"Never mind, Mum. This is Mr. Rogers."

"Mr Bodgers-Mr-Bodgers-Mr Bodgers!" she gabbled. "Pleased-to-eat-you!"

"And I'm most certainly pleased to meet you, Mrs Fox," he said. The woman had gone dewlally! He'd probably get the house off her really cheap.

Hazel was disgusted. His mouth was actually drooling! Dripping!

"I've come to help you!" he shouted.

She wasn't deaf!

"Oh – good-boy! Good-boy! Good-boy!" she squealed. "Can you make vegetable stew, Mr. Dodgers?"

Hazel hated his sickly smile.

"I'm your *bank manager!*" he proclaimed. "And I'm going to buy the house off you, Mrs. Fox. So you can pay off all your debts."

Her mother shuddered and almost collapsed, as if she'd been punched. "No, no, no!" she muttered in a half-strangled cry. "Jeff wouldn't allow that. He's coming back, you know. He hasn't *really* left us, Mr. Stodgy."

Hazel caught her as she sank backwards. "It'll be all right, Mum. It'll be all right," she said. "Mr. Rogers isn't *really* going to buy the house."

He was actually *glowing* with greed. (And Podgers was creeping up the stairs, unseen, to inspect his new bedroom.) "Oh, you don't need to worry," the fat man said. "I've found you a nice little house." He flashed a shiny brochure towards them. "Park Heights!" he announced. *"A very tasteful development of sensible, small properties* – In Sheffield."

"SHEFFIELD!" Hazel boomed, making him jump backwards.

"It will be so convenient for you both," he explained. "You mother needs a job and . . ."

"We're *not* moving to *Sheffield!*" she shouted.

"There will be so much for a young lady to do."

"WE'RE NOT! OKAY? I'm *not* leaving here!"

"Archibald will look after the dogs and —"

There was a squeal of delight from upstairs. "I've *gotta* have this bedroom with the spooky cupboard!" he yelled down. "It's *massive!*"

That was her room.

"I could get all my computer gear in here. No sweat!" he shouted.

Hazel couldn't speak. The thought of that flabby, greasy body in *her* bedroom made her feel faint. She just managed . . . to run outside . . . in time . . . and . . .*vomit!* . . . All down the glinting windscreen of the nice, cream car.

9

Hazel

Friday 10th March

Podgers *wasn't* going to get their house! She wouldn't *let* him! It was morning break and she'd had enough of Toby's *World Skipping Championships*. She'd got too many things to work out, anyway. She pushed on the school door and drifted in. If only she could *think* of something! She'd love to run home and say "Mum! Mum! I've done it! I've got the answer!" Not that her mother would even *hear* what she said. She lived in a sort of trance these days. Hazel couldn't even get her out of bed. She stood still at the thought of her mother, curled up like a hibernating mouse. Sometimes she was all weepy and sometimes all daft and giggly. Perhaps she should take her to the doctor's.

Hazel didn't see two boys come in behind her. She didn't see them whispering and creeping up on her. She just felt a *wham!* in the middle of her back which nearly knocked her over.

"Boys only, in here!" Podgers told her.

"Yeah," his mate Liam sneered. "Girls shouldn't hang about outside our loos!"

"FLASH AND FLESH!" she jeered. "Anyway, *you* shouldn't be in before the bell, either!"

"We're *allowed!*" Liam whined, undoing his new, flashy jacket. "I'm getting changed for the race."

"What race?"

"She doesn't even *know* about it!" Podgers scoffed. "Dumbo-o! Dumbo-o!"

Liam came right up to her and spoke very slowly. "The – mile – race – Mr McGeever – has – been – telling – us – about – all – morning – *Dingbat!*" he said.

"Sounds stupid," she said.

Liam swung his Man United bag at her. "Well, it would to you, wouldn't it?" he said. "You probably run like all girls. Like you're falling to bits!"

He just thought he was the best at *everything*. "I could beat *you* if I wanted to," she said.

"Oh, I bet! Anyway, girls aren't allowed!"

"That's sexist!" She said. She hated that "aren't-I-clever" grin of his. "Girls can do anything boys can do now."

"Right!" they said, grabbing her wrists. "You can come and see our loos, then!"

She couldn't do anything about it. Her feet slid over the tiles and they dragged her through the rattling, crashing doorway. "Pooh!" she said, trying to twist out of their hands. "It stinks in here!"

Podgers had wrapped his arms around her like a wrestler. She hated it. He felt all soft and spongy and warm. *"Get off, you lump! Get off!"* But she couldn't break his grip. He was so heavy against her. She had to walk backwards. "NO!" she said. "NO!" She was *inside* one of their toilet cubicles. And they both squeezed in with her. *"Let me go! Let me go!"* She was pushed and pulled and banged around until she fell over – and was actually *sitting* on one of their toilet pans!

"Yah! Hah!" Liam scoffed. "Winnie the Pooh is having a poo!"

Hazel felt wild – out of control. She jumped up and scrabbed at Liam's face but he dodged away. She whacked into Podgers so hard that he fell over, whimpering, onto the floor.

She had a wonderful, delicious idea!

She pushed his head right down into the pan and flushed the gurgling water all over his head. When he turned round, the water was running all down his face. "You look like a *mop!*" she jeered. "A stinky old *mop!*"

He bawled like a baby and tried to punch her.

"You'll get done for this!" Liam threatened.

But she just laughed, made a grab for him, and chased him out into the playground.

* * *

Year Six trooped through the gate onto the Fair Field. It was the only flat land in the village. Hazel looked around, half-expecting to see the excited dogs, the crowds, the hot-dog stalls and the waving bookies – All the colour and noise you got here when they brought the dogs for the Fell Races.

She saw Podgers glaring at her. You could see he'd been crying. Liam shook his fist at her and Podgers copied.

"Flash and Flesh!" she called at them.

"No – Flash and Flush!" Claire said.

"We just gotta beat Liam!" Toby said.

"Yeah. But he's pretty good," Spinksy told them. "And look at his fancy running shoes."

Liam lifted his foot to show off the spikes. "*Now* we'll see if girls are as good as boys!" he taunted her.

* * *

Running on the flat was easy-peasy! She could have run ahead and overtaken Liam any time she wanted to. She really had to force herself to go slow so that she could stay back with the others.

"Why don't you just go and overtake him?" Toby said, holding his side.

She laughed. "I've got an evil plan," she told him. "I want him to think he's won it. Then I'm gonna WHIZ past him at the end."

"Only one more lap!" Spinksy said. "You'd better start motoring! He's way ahead!"

He was about a quarter of a lap in front. Yeah. She ought to get moving. "Right!" she said. "See you at the finish." She was going to enjoy this. She clenched her fists and started leaping ahead. It felt great to open up and really start running. "Here I come, Mummy's little charm-pot!"

Claire was watching with the others. *"Yes!"* she said. *"Yes!* Hazel-jet has taken off!"

Hazel got right up close to him. She could hear his horrible breathing. And his legs were all wobbly. He'd had it! She loved it when he turned and saw her. She just loved the look on his face.

"No! No! Get back!" he screamed, terrified. He was nearly crying! She felt sort of sorry for him, then.

"Say 'girls are as good as boys' and we can draw," she said down to him.

The spikes in his running shoes were made of a bright, sharp alloy. He was watching her big feet. Watching as they plonked down right beside him. He counted the beats . . . 'One-two-three . . . One-two-three . . . One-two-three . . . *Now!'* He stamped right down as hard as he could on her left foot.

Claire and everyone heard her scream and saw her fall and roll over. Hazel thought she'd stepped on a rat trap!

She pulled her foot up hard and screwed her face up against the pain. She just wanted to cry! Roll into a ball and cry! Inside her head, her father was shouting at her. *"Think, Hazel! Think! Forget your foot! Think! Work it out!"*

She half opened her eyes to slits and looked to see where he was. There was still a half a lap left. She could still catch him. *If* she could run!

Claire was watching. She saw Hazel struggle up onto her feet . . . "Come on, Haze . . !" Hobble a few paces . . . "Come on . . !" Then, sort of *throw* herself forward . . . "She's going . . !" And into her rhythm again. "COME ON, HAZE! COME ON!" she yelled.

He was about twenty metres ahead of her. "Work it out, Hazelnut. Work it out." "But it hurts, Dad." "Forget that. *Think!*"

She pushed on her elbows and started to leap her brilliant, super-girl leaps!

Ten metres . . . Five . . . Two . . . One metre!

"Get back! I'll spike you again!"

"Liam's nearly home!" Podgers said, wobbling with excitement.

Ten paces left. Her feet dug in and hauled her forward.

"It's Liam!"

"Haze. Come on, Haze!"

"Liam!"

"Hazel!"

"Get back! Get back!"

"Hazel! Hazel! Come on!"

"Liam!"

"They're *level!*"

"COME BACK! COME BACK!"

"It's Hazel!"

"No!"

"YES! YES!"

It felt so good! She was in front. No-one could stop her winning. What a feeling! She just *zipped* over the line!

"SUPER-HAZEL!"

She hobbled to a halt and turned to face him. He ran right up to her. "I could beat you if I was as big as you!" he panted. "You're unnatural! A *giant*. Anyone could run if they had legs like *telescopes!*"

"Yeah! *Stethoscopes!*" Podgers copied.

"You two are *pathetic!*" she said.

"Yeah! *MAGNETIC!*" Claire sneered right in Podgers' face.

Hazel felt Mr McGeever's hands guiding her down onto the grass. "Now, lass," he said. "Tell us all your wish."

"What wish?"

He laughed kindly. "You haven't *quite* been with us this week, Hazel, have you?"

Claire pulled a drippy, blood-soaked sock off her foot. "You get a wish," she told her.

"If you win the big final," Toby said.

"In London," Spinksy added.

"What, really? Like in a fairy tale?"

"Yeah. Really, Nutkin. From the Queen."

They both laughed. Claire started walking like the Queen. "Well, I wish my foot didn't hurt, Your Majesty!" Hazel said.

Mr. McGeever winked at her. "You can think of a better wish than that, lass." he urged her, looking over at Podgers.

Then it hit her. Just like that! The *whole world-slamming, universe-shattering idea! Wham!* "Can you ask for *anything?*" she asked, hobbling up to him.

"Course you can," he said, understanding her.

"*Our house then!*" she blurted out. "I wish the Queen to buy our house for us! If I win." It felt great, just saying it.

"YOU CAN'T!" Podgers wailed. "WE'RE HAVING IT!"

"Oh yes, she can," Mr McGeever said. "So long as it's not actually *sold* before the Final – that's the twenty-eighth of August, I believe."

"YOU CAN'T! YOU CAN'T!" he blubbered.

"Anyway," Liam said. "She'll never beat all the other giants in the country. That's *impossible!*"

Hazel laughed. "The only things that are *impossible*, Hazelnut," Father-man had told her, "are the things you can't imagine."

10

Billy

Thursday 9th March

Billy was on the school roof. Right at the very top. Laughing at the stars above and making "V" signs at the world below. He was trying to scramble onto his feet and grab the weather vane on top of the chimney. But, once again, his feet slipped off the pointy ridge and he crashed down onto the hard slates. "Hell and bugger!" he shouted into the night.

Then he had an idea! Which didn't pause in his head but flew straight into his legs and arms. "Commando Billy, leap!" he ordered himself. "Commando Billy, *dive!*"

Instead of trying to drag himself up the bricks, he was going to do a little run along the ridge and launch himself at the chimney – like a goalie making a save.

* * *

Far below in the moonlit playground, Bobby, Billy's twin brother, was waiting in the shadows – exactly in the spot Billy had placed him. Watching, as Billy had said. Staring up at the chimney high above the front of the school. "Bibby! Bibby! Where are oo?" his babyish voice sang in the wind. He heard a thump and a yell as Billy crashed against the chimney. "BIBBY! BIBBY!" he shrieked out, dancing a little circling dance and weeing down his legs.

* * *

"Mission accomplished!" Billy announced, hugging the chimney. He could see Eastwick lighthouse on the coast, sweeping its yellow beam across the fields and farms. "Ship ahoy!" he yelled at it . . . Then he heard Bobby's whimpering and he began searching the shadowy playground for the pale face.

"Bolly stared! Bolly stared!" he heard him cry.

"It's okay, Bobbo. It's okay," he thought-whispered tenderly. "Billy's alright, Bobbo." The special, silent message made Bobby feel safe again. Billy was *never* away from Bobbo. He was always nearby to look after him. Protect him. Bash anyone who laughed at him.

Billy looked up at the clanking weather vane. "Now, Private Billy," he said. "Finish the job."

He hated their Head – Mrs Bottom. She was seriously horrible to him. It had been great creeping into her garden and burgling her washing-line! He felt into his back pocket and pulled out some underwear.

"SAS, *fix bra!*" he ordered himself. "Mrs Balloon-Boob's bra!" He reached up and tied the bra onto the west pointer of the cold iron vane. The wind filled the cups and they flapped outwards and tickled his face. He grinned the grin that people were always telling him to wipe off his face.

"SAS, *fix knickers!*" he laughed, tying them to the east pointer. "Elephant-bum knickers!"

When Billy was excited he was dangerous. He stepped back and punched the air with both fists as if he'd scored a goal. He forgot he was up on a roof! At that exact second he heard the police car and tried to spin himself round to look.

"PEECE!" Bobby yelled, beginning a frantic zig-zag dance. "PEECE! PEECE!"

Billy lost his balance and toppled forward into the blackness . . . *Wham!* He hit the slates. His legs came up and over him. And he rolled and bumped down towards the edge of the roof.

* * *

PC Brian Bolt opened the car door and stepped out into the night.

* * *

"*Pod*, Bibby! *Pod!*" Bobby screamed. They called him Plod.

The guttering scraped across Billy's back as he slid over it and down towards the playground.

* * *

Plod stared up at the roof, trying to get his eyes used to the dark.

* * *

Bobby wet himself again and began shaking.

* * *

Billy smacked down hard into the sandpit, his whole body burning with pain. His breath had been whammed out of him. And stars rushed round above him and made him feel sick.

* * *

Plod ran across the playground to the place where he'd heard the crash. He felt around in the wet sand . . . But he couldn't find anything.

* * *

Billy was used to pain. He was always in fights. And he was always bashing himself. When he'd seen Plod racing towards him, he'd jumped up without any thought . . . and dodged away around the corner.

* * *

Plod looked up. The gutter was broken and swinging dangerously. A loose slate slipped and fell beside him.

* * *

"Bobbo, it's me," Billy whispered.

"Bibby! Bibby!"

The two boys hugged in the dark corner beside the bike shed.

"Come on. We gotta get away." Billy took Bobby's hand and led him across the school field.

* * *

PC Brian Bolt sighed. "The Buttons again," he said. "I just hope it wasn't Billy." Plod liked his job. He liked the village. And he liked the Buttons – Sharon and Kevin and their *eighteen* children. But he felt so sorry for Billy.

* * *

They followed the moonlit tracks over the common and came to the back of the council houses. They slipped through the gate and picked their way across their "back garden" – a jungle of giant nettles, car engines, old tyres and oil drums. Billy looked up at the two houses and listened. The District Council had knocked numbers 42 and 44 Heath View into one house when Kylie (Number 8) had been born. "It's okay, Bobbo. Come on," he said. "We'll go in the back."

Billy (Number 6A) and Bobby (6B) crept carefully into the kitchen of Number 42. Number 44's kitchen was now a downstairs bedroom for Sindy (Number 1) and Terri-Anne-Louise (Number 3). Billy blinked against the room's sudden brightness and tried to hide his cut hands. His Ma was sitting at the table doing *six million* jobs at once with her *eight arms!* "Octo-Mum does it again!" Billy grinned, watching.

She was feeding Garth (Number 17) on her lap. Holding down Terry-the-Terror (Number 13) with *one finger!* And helping Dean-the-Dream (Number 5) and Bart (Number 9) with their yo-yo's. *All at once!*

"Me and Bobby have just set light to Chapel Farm, Ma," Billy told her.

"Good boys. Good boys," she said, jabbing a spoonful of sicky-stuff into Garth's mouth while he was yawning.

"And we've sunk the lifeboat at Eastwick."

"Oh, well done," she told them between yo-yo doggie-walks.

Billy's grin was set hard on his face. But he wasn't grinning inside. Inside, he was just wishing that he could have her all to himself. Or that she'd at least *talk* to him. It was stupid . . . but he wished *he* could be sitting on her lap like Garth. "Come on, Bobbo! We gotta hide. Before Plod comes!" he said.

They hurried past the fridges and the crisp-bin and into Number 42 dining-room. The table had been stood on end and Kevin Button, their father, was bent over a Ford Escort engine in pieces on the floor. "Now, where's that gasket?" he wondered, not noticing four legs picking their way through a muddle of engine parts and a puddle of sludgy oil on the carpet.

Where could they hide? "In nair! In nair!" Bobby said

64

pointing into Number 42 lounge. Billy looked in. There was a stack of bodies piled up on the couch and a *mountain* on the floor! All hypnotised by a car-chase on the telly.

"Nah! Upstairs," he decided.

They tip-toed through the hall towards the bottom of the stairs. And it was like he'd been waiting there for them! Just as they passed the front door it shook as if a *giant* was thumping it! And Plod's face was pushed up against the little window, peering in.

Bobby screamed and hid his head in Billy's back.

Billy's grin widened. And his hands made their own decision. They grabbed the door and yanked it wide open. He liked Plod. He was the only one who ever really talked to him. And *listened*. But he still cheeked him: "Don't tell us, Inspector. There's been a murder down at the vicarage!"

"What you been doing tonight, Billy?" he asked in that Father-Christmassy voice of his.

"Telly!" Billy snapped.

"Telly? What was on?"

"Film!"

Plod twisted Billy round and nodded at the school-roof slime swiped across his back.

"*Dirty* film!" Billy joked. "I been *here!* Ask my mum!"

Plod put his hands on Billy's shoulders and looked down into his eyes. "I hate to remind you, Billy," he said. "But you know that the magistrates issued a Court Order on you, don't you? After you smashed all those windows." He waited but Billy just kept grinning.

"Been *here!*" he said. "Ask *anyone!*"

"Billy, that Court Order was a *last warning*. You know that. And Jane knows that."

Billy groaned. *Jane! Cardboard Jane* – his social worker.

She couldn't *wait* to get him into her precious children's home.

"I just hope it wasn't you on the school roof tonight, Billy. I really do."

"It wasn't! *Promise!* On my hamster's life . . !"

He watched Plod go up the path . . . back to that brilliant house . . . where Mrs Plod had given him his tea once . . . just him and Bobbo alone.

Then they *did* go and hide. They ran upstairs, climbed the rickety wall-ladder and clambered through the trapdoor into their loft-room – their owl's nest, high in the night . . . Lovely! Safe! The room smelt of mice and straw. And crumbly old roof tiles. And Bobby's wee. The light didn't work so they felt their way through the dark and into the bottom bunk . . . and lay cuddled together . . . staring up through the skylight at the stars.

Billy made this bed every morning. And, two or three times a week, he would have to bundle the bottom sheet into Number 44 washing machine. He snuggled tight against Bobby's back. "It wouldn't be *too bad* in a children's home, Bobbo," he said. "We might have some fun!"

Bobby didn't answer. His eyes were wide open. Staring at a terrifying tomorrow. He didn't even notice the warm wee dribbling down into the mattress.

11

Billy

Friday 10th March

The whole school was in the front playground, laughing and pointing up at the weather vane. Where a pair of bulging white bloomers and a huge bra were twizzling and twisting in the wind.

"Jimminy-scrimminy! How the heck did they get up there?" Ben Coull asked.

"Flippin' angel left them there, I expect!" Joe Gildersleeves told him.

"Bloomin' fat angel!"

Billy's grin almost cut his head in half! "I might know! I might know!" he blabbered.

"You don't know *anything*, Button!" Ben Coull scoffed. "'Cept how to pinch things and demolish things!"

"He don't even know how to *read!*" Joe laughed.

Billy's grin had disappeared.

Joe pointed up at the underwear. "At least they're clean!" he told everyone. "Not all stained and smelly like *Wobby Wutton's!*"

Billy put an arm round Bobby's shoulder.

"Heck, he stinks today!" Ben said. "Pooh! SMELLY BUTTON! SMELLY BUTTON! BOLLY-BELLY-SMELLY BUTTON!"

Without a millisecond's thought, Billy spun round and sunk his fist hard into Ben Coull's stomach – *"Oof!"* he went down – and he managed to kick Joe in the bum before the lout ran away.

The school bell stopped them. *"Clang! Clang!"* Everyone began lining up to go in. Mrs Bottom stood on the school step glaring at them as if they were all murderers or something!

"STAND STILL!" she commanded.

A few of the little ones were still pointing.

"Put your hands *down!*" she screamed.

"But *Miss!*"

"DOWN I said!"

Billy couldn't *wait* for her to see her own knickers dancing above the school. "She'll probably burst – POW!" he muttered in the silence.

"Now you know we're going to have our Wishing Race this morning," she told them all. What a *stupid* idea! she thought. Children today have far too much without encouraging them to wish for *more!* And she had *quite* enough to do today without having to organise a silly race. She had to see PC Bolt about her missing undies for one thing. And there was that *awful* School Inspector's Report to deal with. She *must* stop it getting into the newspapers!

"Billy Button! Take that stupid grin off your face, boy!" she screamed. If only Billy Button hadn't been in school the week the inspectors had come. "BILLY BUTTON! Will you stand STILL in the line!"

"Old Bag!" Billy muttered.

"WHAT?"

"The new *flag*, Miss. Just admiring your new school flag."

She stepped down very, very daintily, as if she didn't want to actually *touch* any of them. She had to squint against the sun to see what they were all looking at. "O-oh! O-oh! How could anyone? How could *anyone?*"

Billy was laughing so much he nearly fell over. "How could anyone wear such baggy old knickers?" he called out. He loved the way they all stared at him. "Why don't you leave 'em up there, Miss? We can tell how strong the wind is by how big the bum gets!" But no-one laughed.

"BILLY BUTTON!" she screamed, making the infants jump.

"Someone must have a huge old *ARSE!*" he said. "And bloomin' great floppy *BOOBS!*"

"O-oh! O-oh!"

He didn't think what he was saying. "They're old Bottom's knickers," he told everyone around him. "They're off her line. Look at the size of 'em!"

"MISS! MISS!" they all hissed. "MISS! MISS! MISS!"

"They sound like a load of snakes!" he told Bobby.

Ben Coull was still holding his stomach. "It was Billy Button, Miss!" he said. "Button did it!"

"I might have known!" she spat the words at Billy as if she'd like to *kill* him!

Everyone turned to watch a car edging into the playground. "PEECE!" Bobby said. "POD!"

When Billy turned back, Mrs Bottom was charging at him, her face all twisted and wild. Billy yelped as her finger-nails sank into his arm. "You WICKED boy!" she boomed, shaking him. "You *wicked, evil* boy!"

Bobbo was dancing around and bawling, helpless to help his brother. Billy tried to grab his hand but he couldn't. Everyone was getting squashed. They all wanted to see Button getting it from Miss.

It was PC Bolt who pulled the wild woman away from Billy. She was snorting and exhausted. "Take him away Constable!" she yelled. "*Into Care!* Where he belongs."

"YEAH! YEAH! INTO CARE!" the kids cheered.

Billy could feel Bobby moaning and sobbing in his arms. He was grinning his "couldn't care less" grin. "It's okay, Bobbo. It's okay," he reassured. "You'll come with me."

"*He most certainly will not!*" Mrs Bottom said triumphantly. "*He* will go to a *special* school. Where there are other children like him!"

The kids were chanting:

"WOBBY WUTTON!

WOBBY WUTTON!

BYE!

BYE!

BYE!

WOBBY WUTTON!

WOBBY WUTTON!

BYE!

BYE!

BYE!"

Billy just stared at everyone. *Nobody* would take him away from Bobbo! *No-one* could be that cruel! "Ple-ease," he pleaded. He would *never* forget that look on Mrs Bottom's face – all hard and happy – as she marched up and yanked Bobby away from him. He was just too dazed to do anything. "No-o-o-o-o! No-o-o-o-o! Ple-ea-ease!" he wailed, trying to grab Bobbo back.

But Plod had a firm grip on Billy's arm. "It'll be okay Billy. It'll be okay, son," he tried to comfort. "You'll like it in the home,"

Billy tugged like a mad thing and sort of dived free.

But Plod swung a big arm round his tummy and lifted him off the ground.

Billy rolled along the arm and crashed down onto the hard playground.

Plod grabbed his shirt!

Billy dived back between Plod's legs, breaking his grip. As he scrambled to his feet he bashed Plod on the bum and sent him flying into Mrs Bottom as if they were in love!

Billy didn't see any of that. He was sprinting towards the bottom gate like a cheetah!

"BIBBY! BIBBY!" he heard Bobbo calling. But he had to keep going.

12

Billy

Friday 10th March

Plod set a trap for Billy. He sat Bobby down on a chair in the middle of the school field. Then he squeezed himself into the tiny PE shed . . . and waited . . . for Billy to come to his brother . . . sitting there, all alone, in the open. The rest of the school were lined up in neat rows, waiting for the Wishing Race to begin.

* * *

Billy ran onto the marsh and hid in their grassy den.But after a long, quiet time he got fed up and wandered over to the allotments . . . Someone had left a big fork out and he played spearing scarecrows. Then he began drifting back towards school . . . He couldn't forget Bobbo's screams and he began hurrying . . . then running.

* * *

He pulled the school door open really slowly . . . Silence! Not one single voice! "Flippin' Nora!" he said. "They've *all* run off. Serves the old bag right!" Then he remembered that Wishing Race thing and sneaked round to the field.

They were all sitting there like creepy little goody-goodies and the old dragon was bossing the runners about. "Plonkers!" Billy whispered, watching her poke them and push them into a starting line.

Then he saw Bobbo. Sitting by himself. Out in the open. Where he could go in and snatch him – Easy! "Bobbo! Billy's here!" he thought-shouted. Bobby turned and looked around – first at the little PE shed – then at the gate . . . No Billy. So he turned back to watch the race.

Billy scrabbed some dirt up and rubbed it into his face like a real commando and crawled through the gate, his radar eyes scanning the field for danger.

Plod couldn't believe his eyes! There was Billy crawling towards him! He climbed over a stack of rubbery footballs and opened the door a tiny bit.

Mrs Bottom was calling out to the runners. "A straight line! A *straight line!* That's simple enough, surely!"

"Boss-Bum!" Billy muttered into the grass. He was half-way now. Just past the PE shed. "Bobbo! Bobbo!" he thought-called.

Bobbo spun round . . . but he looked terrified. *"BIBBY WUN! BIBBY WUN!"* he screamed at him.

Billy turned to see what Bobbo was looking at. Plod racing towards him! In less than a second he was up on his feet and running.

"Are you ready, now?" Mrs Bottom nagged. "ON YOUR MARKS!"

Brian Bolt was a champion runner. He trained every week with the "Suffolk Greyhounds" and he'd even run for the English Police. He'd soon catch the lad. No problem . . . except . . . except . . . *Blimey!* The little swizzer was *gaining* on him!

Billy ran right past Bobby, past the rest of the school and out onto the track.

"GET SET!"

"The boy's *bionic!*" Plod grinned, stopping beside Bobby.

"GO!" The runners leapt forward and Mrs Bottom's eyes followed them towards the bend . . . Then something else flashed past her. "*Button! Billy Button!*" she croaked, staggering.

Someone was running at him, trying to grab him. He dodged and she fell over. It was Jane! The stick insect! Come to take him away. "Serves you rights! You anorexic spider!" Billy jeered, swerving round some other runners.

"Get back, Button!" Ben Coull snapped at him. "This is the Wishing Race."

"What *he* needs is a *washing* race!" Joe laughed.

"Yeah. Mess off, Button!"

"I could beat you lot!" he yelled at them. "A runny snout runs faster than you lot!" He tucked his chin in and started running really hard, his eyes fixed on the red marker cones.

Plod was amazed. The boy ran like a champion. He had real style. "He's good, Bobby," he said. "Billy's very good."

They were all screaming and hopping up and down:

"THOM-AS! THOM-AS!"

"BEN COULL! BEN COULL!"

"JEM-MA!"

Mrs Bottom flapped her arms at them desperately as if they were a fire she couldn't put out. In the end she gave up and sat down heavily. Plod laughed . . .

It was something out on the field that made them sit down, one by one . . . in silence . . . and stare . . . A lean scruffy figure, zooming along like a motorised scarecrow.

Plod dropped his cap and watched with his mouth open.

Billy ran past them like a grin on legs! He loved it! Everyone watching him. Way out in front of the other doodle-heads. Brilliant! He wiggled his bum and raised his arms in a sort of salute.

Kirsty Lomas stood up alone above the others. She hated the way everyone was always horrible to Billy. Normally she kept quiet but now she yelled: "BIL-LY! BIL-LY! BIL-LY!" People stared at her as if she'd suddenly started speaking Martian! Then her little gang stood up around her.

"BIL-LY! BIL-LY!" they chanted.

Bobby heard it and laughed up into Plod's face. "BIB-BY! BIB-BY!" he copied.

Billy heard it too and he did a sort of a sexy twirl and a skip for them. He'd never, ever felt so happy in all his life. It was fantastic. He ran even faster!

"Here he comes!" Kirsty said. He looked so sleek. Slicing the air and flying towards the finish.

"BIBBY-WIN! BIBBY-WIN!" Bobby yelled.

Mrs Bottom screamed a little mouse of a scream in disbelief. Billy leapt across the finish and threw himself in a victory roll on the grass for everyone to see.

He was on his back, his arms spread, grinning. He closed his eyes tight. He wanted to keep the feeling *in*. He wanted to dream it all, over and over again . . . He'd forgotten that they were after him! Suddenly, people were falling on him and holding him down.

"*Got you!*" Mrs Bottom said.

"*At last!*" Cardboard Jane said triumphantly. She had her knees on his shoulders. They were like spikes!

Billy felt about a *million* hands pulling at him and they began dragging and bumping him across the grass towards her car. All he could see were legs and bums. "Hang on!" he yelled at them. "Mind me body!"

Bobby was hopping about around them and kicking anyone he could get to.

Ben Coull got down so close to Billy he could feel his spit. *"I win, Button!"* he sneered. "'Cos they're taking *you* away!"

"Leave him!" Kirsty shouted, trying to pull him off and help Bobby at the same time.

Plod stretched up over the heads and saw them pull Billy onto his feet and try to stuff him into the little Fiat. They looked like they were going to *murder* him! He couldn't wait any longer. He just pushed himself into the mob. "HOLD ON A MINUTE!" he roared. "STAND BACK EVERYONE! I'LL DEAL WITH BILLY BUTTON!"

Thank God! Billy felt the hands relax and leave him. Then Plod appeared and put a hand on his shoulder. He couldn't *believe* what Plod said to Mrs Bottom: "Are you *sure* you want to sent young Billy into care?" he asked her.

Super-Plod to the rescue!

"Yes, I am! Quite *quite* sure!" she said. "He's a wicked, wicked boy!"

Blimey! They could bottle the look on her face for *rat poison!*" Then Cardboard Jane stuck *her* nose in! "There is no *question*!" she said in her birdy voice. "The boy *has* to go into care!"

Plod turned to Billy and lifted him up *on top* of her car. "See this lad?" he said to everyone. "He could be a *champion*, he could."

"HUH! I don't think so!" Mrs Bottom said.

"Oh yes, he could," Plod insisted. "We could have a future Olympic champion right here in the village. Believe me. This boy is a truly great runner!"

Billy felt people looking at him in a different way. "Told you, didn't I?" Kirsty said.

Mrs Bottom came right up to Billy. He thought she was

going to hit him. But she looked for a long moment into his eyes, then she started to examine him closely. She poked his legs as if she was testing an old chicken in Sainsbury's! She felt his hard muscles. "You mean *this boy* . . . *this boy* . . . could actually *win* the whole Wishing Race?" she asked.

"Billy Button could beat anyone his age in the entire country! Yes, I'm sure of it," Plod told them all.

Billy glowed and held his arms wide to show them that the wonderful Billy Button was actually here amongst them.

"And the school could be *famous,* Mrs Bottom," Plod went on.

"*Famous?*" she repeated. "What, in the newspapers?"

"Oh, the papers, yes. And the television." He gave her a huge wink. "No-one would ever mention that old School Inspector's report again!" he said.

Cardboard Jane waved a sheet of paper. "I've got this Court Order here," she said. "Billy's *got* to go into care!"

Plod whipped it out of her hand and slipped it into his pocket, real quick! "I think we can forget *that* for a little while!" he said. "Billy could sort of be in *our* care, *here*. He could come running with me. You could watch him at school, Mrs Bottom. And I could have a word with his parents as well . . ."

"We'll help!" Kirsty said, giving Billy a sort of film-star smile that made him feel funny. She came right up close to him and delivered Bobby. Billy jumped down. It felt so good to hold onto Bobbo again. Sort of safe. And warm. "You could be in *our* gang, Billy," Kirsty said.

"But this boy would *never* be a champion, Constable," Mrs Bottom told him. "He's the *laziest* boy in the school! He can't even read! He'd never *work* at anything!"

Billy twisted round to her. *"Yes I would!"* he insisted.

"I'd train really hard, Miss. Properly – you know. Whatever Plod – I mean Constable Bolt – said." All he wanted to do was run and run and run! Win races and win races and win races. He'd do *anything!*

"We-ell . . ." Mrs Bottom said. "Er . . . We-ell . . . Just for a time, perhaps . . . While he's still in that Wishing Race . . . But as soon as he's knocked out of it, he's *off! Into the children's home!* Is that clear, Constable?"

"It's a deal, Miss!" Billy said, shaking her hand hard.

13

Buckingham Palace

Monday 28th August

The Queen slipped out onto the balcony at the front of the palace. It was going to be hot. There was already a golden heat haze shimmering over her capital. Out beyond her black and gold gates, workmen were hammering and sawing. She couldn't *wait* for it all to begin! Some days were just plain boring. But *this* one! This one she'd looked forward to for months. Once again, she read the names of the sixteen children and their wishes, nodding and smiling thoughtfully.

Outside in the road, Charlie Wilson, track designer and Chief Race Steward, looked around at his work. "Brilliant, Charlie! Fantastic! Perhaps you'll get a knighthood, son – 'Sir Charles Wilson' . . . Well, maybe not." But it *was* looking good. When he'd arrived yesterday, traffic had been bombing up The Mall and around this roundabout like bank holiday dodgems! And now there was a four-lane running track painted on the road around it. And a ring of wooden stands all around the edge, for the ten thousand spectators! *And* a Royal Box! "Magic, Charlie. Sheer magic, my son."

When he saw the sixteen runners getting out of the coach he knew the countdown had begun. He'd met them all at the Royal Kingston Hotel over the weekend. They'd been treated to a right royal knees-up! For three days! *And* all their families! *And* a friend each! . . He began leading them around the track. Fifteen walking. One in a wheelchair.

The blond boy from Kent was pointing up at the big screens above the roundabout. "Hey! What are they for?" he asked Charlie.

"Live TV," Charlie told him. "So the crowd can see all the race."

The tiny Welsh boy saw a camera pointed down at them and did some cartwheels. They all laughed when it appeared on the big screens.

Streak, the lad from Sunderland, was pushing the wheelchair. Isaac had told his Ma he wanted to save his energy for the races, so could he have one? He hadn't told her that, one morning, he'd discovered that he could hardly walk! She didn't know that, because he could still run. Even faster than before! As his illness had got worse his running had got better! The wicked attacks he got these days jerked his legs out so hard he ran like a super-charged turbo-jet! All the London papers called him "Miracle Boy". He'd won his Area Race in the park. His North London race beside that motorway. And his All-London Final at Crystal Palace Stadium. He was famous! But he knew his body had almost had it . . . .

He didn't care – as long as he could get his Ma to Jamaica. And he would! Yes sir! By Jesus's beard, he would . . ! He listened hard to what Mr Wilson was telling them.

"You'll all run this morning," he began. "There'll be four semi-finals, starting at eleven o'clock. Four of you in each one . . ." They were all listening. The crowd was filling up. They'd stopped larking around. "The four winners will run in the final, this afternoon."

A big man in a stripy suit and clip-cloppy shoes

marched across to them. He taught them how to bow and curtsy – and when to call the Queen "Your Highness" and when to just say "Ma'am". Then he led them up the steps to the Royal Box to practice receiving their medals.

Hazel liked the scarlet cushion the Queen would sit on. And she liked all the purple and gold silk. And the little flags strung along the fringe of the roof. She looked across to the left where the families were beginning to take their seats. Claire stood up and waved her sixteen good luck teddies. How the heck had they managed to get her mother to London? She hadn't been out of bed for three months! The two of them had packed everything into crates by themselves. Soon, they'd know the moving date. They hadn't been to Sheffield *once* to look at Number 24 Sycamore Close.

If only she could win today! If only she could be like Sneezy who'd won four fell races straight off! She'd won her Area Race round Scraggy Hill. She'd won at Sheffield. And she'd won the North West Regional Final in Manchester. Please! Please! Please! Just two more races!

At ten-forty precisely Charlie Wilson lined them up in front of the Royal Box. "Hands behind your back. That's it. With your right hand holding your left wrist. Good soldiers! Good soldiers!"

Billy stood up really straight with his chest out and his chin up like an SAS commando! He could see Cardboard Jane crawling towards her seat behind his mother. She'd followed him to every race, the frog-face! She'd even turned up at Glemham Hall Fete for the Suffolk Finals – Just hoping he'd lose. But he hadn't. He'd won every time. "What a champ you are, Billy-Boy!" he thought. Plod had driven him off to the track every week. And he'd run round the village every day. Run, run, run! That's all he did. He loved it. If running was a girl he'd marry it . . ! Jane glared down at him and he gave her the middle finger.

Some TV bloke was working his way along the line with a microphone. "You're Billy Button, the twin, aren't you?" he asked.

Billy grinned at the camera. "Yeah, I think so," he said. "Or I might be the next King of England – Dunno!"

"I believe you can be quite a naughty boy, Billy, can't you?"

"What me? Not me, mister. I'm an angel, I am. Here – Wanna see my wings?"

The man laughed and moved on . . . "Actually," Billy thought, "I have been a bit of an old angel lately. I ain't been in trouble for ages!" He couldn't work out why he felt so different these days. Why he never wanted to steal now. Or hurt people. Or do crazy things. "You're getting boring and middle-aged, Billy Boy!"

He felt Bobby calling him and when he looked up into the stand he was going bonkers waving. He looked so happy. Like he was going to a party! The whole family – all nineteen, and Plod – started waving. Billy was their *star* now. His Ma smiled her biggest, warmest smile for him. It made him feel so good, so safe. It was a new feeling he'd never known before that summer. He *never* wanted to be away from her now. He gave her that double-wink they were always doing to each other.

Charlie Wilson's stadium was jam-packed full and they heard the crowd sort of moan "Oh-oh! Oh-oh!" when the royal coach rocked its way out onto the track. Billy thought the giant white horses were going to trample him! The coach was real gold – and right there in front of him. He could have *touched* it! Four royal trumpeters jumped down and raised their tasselled trumpets. "Blimey!" Billy said. "Mind me ears will y'!" A little heart-shaped door opened and the Queen stepped down, real close, her white dress crackling, her jewels sparkling. "Got any spares?" Billy joked. Prince Philip straightened his Admiral-of-the-Fleet's cap and gave Billy a look.

"May I introduce Isaac Johansen, Your Majesty," Charlie Wilson said. Isaac did his best to bow sitting in the wheelchair and the Queen shook his hand. "I know all about you, young man," she said. She bent close and whispered in his ear. "I'll be cheering for you, Isaac," she said, "I *will! You* can make *my* wish come true!" Her eyes sparkled like jewels and he knew why she was a queen.

Sylvia waited her turn. Someone had stood up on their seat. They were bowing really low and then holding their nose up snooty-high like a Queen. *Bernie!* How the diddly-poo did *she* get in here? And in the family stand!

Sylvia had been living two lives all summer. They had this place behind the caretaker's incinerator where they met after school while the teachers had meetings. They made up loads of mad acts. Dancing. Singing. All sorts. She loved it. Bernie would do her work for her and, before she left, she'd make the oath of the Sisterhood! – "Blood sisters forever!" Then she'd promise Bernie she'd tell them as soon as she got back. She wasn't gonna be bossed about anymore!

But when she got back to them, she was her old self again. Frightened. Obedient. Running more. Studying more. Imprisoned more. Although, sometimes, she would look at them and say it in her head.

"I've seen you before," the Queen told her. "In the Midlands Final – At the Canal-Boat Centre – On television. Do you remember Philip?" she said, turning to her husband. "You were very good. Very *professional*."

"Th-thank you M-Ma'am – er – Your M-Majesty." Sylvia heard her own words echoing from the big screen behind her.

"I *do* hope you get your wish." The crowd were listening to the royal words. Bernie was absolutely still, staring at her. "Broom Bank is *such* a good school. It's good to know there are young people willing to *work hard* – Isn't it Philip?"

Bernie had disappeared. Slumped down onto her seat in shock! Above her, Sylvia could see her parents looking worried, their faces hard and stiff. They were *terrified* she might not win. And beside them, instead of "a friend", they'd brought Sir Norman Hart-Davis, Principal of Broom Bank. Sylvia wondered if he'd been cut from stone!

The Queen took her seat.

The Band of the Royal Fusiliers played the National Anthem.

Charlie Wilson led them over towards the middle and off the track. Four of them were led away for the first semi-final.

14

The Semi-Finals

The Queen looked down at the four runners waiting nervously in their white vests. Charlie Wilson's voice crackled from a loudspeaker and she checked her list of names.

"In lane one, from the Highlands of Scotland, Malcolm Dudley. In lane two, from Exeter in Devon, Penny Wallis. In lane three, from Sunderland, Tom Bright. And on the outside, in lane four, Isaac Johansen from right here in London." The packed crowd cheered all the names, then there was a hush as they waited for the start.

Mishah was clenching her fists so tight her finger-nails were cutting into her skin. "GO, EYE-SUCKER. GO!" she yelled at him as they spurted forward. Nobody knew what a *whiz-bang of a runner* he'd turned into! But *now* they'd see! *Now* they'd know!

"Oh, he *can* run, Philip!" the Queen said.

Philip chuckled. "He looks a bit like a clockwork chicken, Lilibet," he told his wife. Then his mouth fell open and he stared. "But just look at him *go!* He's *miles* ahead!"

Isaac felt as if he was riding a rocket! His Number Sevens whirred beside him. He just skimmed over the ground, *zooming* ahead. It felt so good.

Tom Bright, "Streak", was in second place. He just

shook his head at the sight of Isaac racing away from him at *unbelievable* speed. "He's not *real!*"

"*Oh, Johansen's strolling it!*" David Coleman, the TV commentator, said out of the big screens.

Florrie Johansen struggled to her feet and squeezed her way along the row, her large bottom almost squashing Walter Starr. When she got down to the front she had to lean on the barrier to get her breath.

Isaac flew through the tape.

"He's done it! He's done it!" the Queen said, grabbing Prince Philip's knee.

Mishah leapt off her seat, kneeing Cardboard Jane in the back. "YO-YO JO-HANSEN!" she chanted.

Isaac scrambled to a halt in front of his Ma. The world had gone dark and his head was spinning and he grabbed the barrier too. The nerves in his legs were still blazing and he swore and screwed up his face.

"Ma-boy! Ma sweet hero-boy!" she said to him.

He could hear the crackling in her voice. He could see how white she looked. "You okay, Ma?" he gasped.

"Sure ah am, boy! Sure ah am! An' what was Queen Elizabeth a-whisperin' about, Issy? Yo ain't keepin' secrets from yo' Ma is y' boy?"

He could tell her now. He'd almost won it, hadn't he? He'd dreamed about this moment for ages. He looked into her face and he found it hard to speak. "Jamaica, Ma!" he said proudly. "I'm takin' you t' Jamaica t' see Granpa George. An' f' a real long holiday in the sun!"

Look at that face! His Ma was a girl again! "Y' hear that, Queenie?" she called up to the Royal Box. "Ma boy! He's gonna take me t' see ma daddy!"

* * *

Hazel watched the stewards as they came into the pen for the next four runners. She tugged at a finger-nail with her teeth. *Not me! Please! Not yet! I'm not ready!* The short one with the pointy beard caught her eye and came over. *No!*

"Hazel Fox?"

"No! . . Yes!"

He laughed. "Come on. You'll be okay."

She kissed her fingers a big smackeroo kiss and touched them on her new trainers for luck – Nineteen pounds, ninety five out of her precious house-keeping money!

Claire thought Pippy Fox looked about as lively as a sack of potatoes! Sitting there, all lollopy and gormless! She took hold of her head and lifted it up. "The race is *that* way!" she said. "Look, They've started."

When they broke out of their lanes, Hazel elbowed her way into the lead. "She's so tall," the Queen said. "She has such long legs."

"And the Welsh chappie is so minuscule!" Prince Philip replied. "He looks like a little corgi running behind her."

Hazel could *feel* him there. She could hear his breathing and his little grunts. She knew what was going to happen next but she couldn't do anything about it. She saw him move out and around her – and he *slid* past. "Oh no!" she said. "Come on! Oh no!"

She felt stuck! Like something was holding her back.

"That Welsh boyo is all muscle" David Coleman said. *"He's pulled right away from Fox, now!"*

Podgers and Liam had a surprise for Hazel. They'd made a banner and they were frantically trying to unwrap it.

"COME ON, LADDER-LEGS!" Claire screamed. "She's too polite – letting everyone go in front! . . Oh, *poo!* She's last, now. Look, Mrs F."

But Hazel's mum had something else on her mind. She

was the only person standing up and staring out the *back* of the stand. "Buckingham Palace," she said dreamily, "and St James's Park."

"She speaks! She speaks!" Claire was amazed. "Someone's switched her on again!"

"It's so romantic here, Jeff," she said. "I'm so glad we came to London for our honeymoon."

Hazel was desperate. "What would Father-man say . . ?" She couldn't remember. "What would *he* tell me to do . . ?" She didn't know.

"He's very good," the Queen said.

"I think he could win the whole thing," Philip told her. "This is the last lap, isn't it?"

Podgers saw Hazel coming round the bend. "Ready?" he asked Liam.

"Yeah. NOW!" Up went the red and white banner. Above everyone's head.

"Looks like you're on your own, now, Hazelnut," she told herself. "All right then! Come on! *No giving up . . !*" There was a big banner at the front of the stand: *"MOVING DAY IS TOMORROW!"* it said. *"GET OUT OF MY BEDROOM!"*

Hazel screamed and almost stopped. *Podgers and Liam,* the stupid moon-faces, were laughing like *idiots*. She had *never ever* been so angry. "I'M NOT MOVING! I'M NOT!" she screamed. "It's my *bedroom!*" Her running became wild and violent. She started kicking and stamping the track real hard.

David Coleman sounded surprised. *"Fox isn't out of it after all. She's trying to catch them. She's not last anymore."*

"HAZEL NUTKIN!" Claire bellowed, making Garth (Number 17) howl – "COME ON YOU LITTLE YORKSHIRE TERRIER!"

The Queen stiffened and jabbed Philip with an elbow. "Mind my bad arm," he said.

"Look at her! Just look at her, darling. How brave she is!"

Hazel was running as if she was chasing someone she wanted to *murder.* Her hands were scrabbing at the air and she was screeching out of control. She didn't know *what* she was doing!

David Coleman's voice rose in excitement. *"Just look at Fox in second place! She'd going like a train! Literally bombing along! I've never seen anything like it! But she can't stop Rhodri Jones. Jones is going to win it . . . No, Fox. She's gone past him! . . But Jones has come back! It's Jones! Yes, Jones . . . Fox! . . Jones! . . FOX! FOX! FOX WINS IT! WHAT A RACE!"*

Podgers punched his father in the stomach and bawled like a baby. "SHE WON! SHE WON!" he cried.

"Never mind, Archibald. She's really worn herself out. She'll never run like that, this afternoon. She's blown it."

"SUPER-NUT! SUPER-NUT! She did it, Mrs F!"

But Pippy Fox was miles away. "Shall we go on the river tonight, Jeffrey?" she murmered. "For a meal on one of those floating restaurants they have on the Thames . . ! Oh, I do love you, Jeffrey!"

* * *

Billy was second. But he couldn't care less! He could catch the posh boy any time he wanted to. "I say, *Herbert!*" he called out to him. "Watch out for that rather smelly fellow behind you, old thing!"

Sharon Button watched the two boys racing toward the end of their third lap. "BUTTONS ARISE!" she ordered, snatching *Engine Parts Monthly* from Kevin.

The Queen's eyes bulged as fifteen children, two babies in nappies, a fat mother, a greasy father and a policeman stood up and began chanting: "OUR BILLY! OUR BILLY!"

Billy did a sexy little wiggle for them and waved. A pity Cardboard Jane had to *spoil* it! She was behind them, waving that horrible Court Order thing at him! *Two* fingers for her this time!

The Queen looked away. Prince Philip tutted.

"That young man really is a character," David Coleman was saying from the big screen. *"But he'll have to start taking this race seriously – Or he'll lose it."*

Kevin nudged Sharon. "'E's got 'is foot on the old accelerator now, love!" he said. "'E's gonna overtake that stainless-steel male model in a sec!"

"Button's catching Gaythorne-Hardy! He's going to pass him!"

Billy grinned. "Move over, old bean, won't you," he asked politely. "There's a good little posh boy."

"OUR BILLY! OUR BILLY!" The Buttons chanted.

"BIL-LY BUTTON! BIL-LY BUTTON!" the school shouted.

"He's going to win, Philip! . . He HAS! . . Oh-oh, he *winked* at me!"

Philip tutted again.

"Well there's a cheeky chappie!" David Coleman said. *"But we're looking at a serious candidate for the Wishing Race Champion. No doubt about that!"*

Cardboard Jane looked like someone had pinched all her blood! Billy laughed at her and flopped down against the barrier . . . Who was that up on the big screen? "Oh no! Oh no!"

"So you're Billy Button's headmistress, are you?" the interviewer was asking.

She looked *embarrassed!* Really uncomfortable! "Er . . . yes . . . yes," she admitted.

"I hear he can be a bit of a scamp?"

Go on! Tell 'em! Tell the whole country! Here's your chance, Dirty Bottom!

Mrs Bottom looked thoughtful. "Actually," she said, "He's not been in any trouble lately . . . In fact," she realised, "he's not *really* been in trouble since he started this running with PC Plod – er, Bolt."

Blimey! She's smiling!

"To tell you the truth, he's been quite a good boy!"

She actually *laughed*. And for a moment, the old baggage turned into a person!

"What's that young man laughing at now?" David Coleman wondered. *"He certainly looks pleased about something!"*

* * *

Sylvia walked out onto the track very slowly. Her hands were sweating. Her eyes fixed down on her feet. She could *feel* them watching her.

It was such a relief when the race actually started. She gave them one glance as she shot away. She wished she hadn't! They were glaring at her. Their faces full of fear, cool Sir Norman beside them.

At least her running was good today. It should be after all that *torture*. She wanted to race ahead. But she controlled herself. Held herself back. Just in front of the group.

"What's she up to?" Walter Starr asked.

"Don't worry," his wife said, not taking her eyes off her. "We know what we're doing."

"What an athlete this young lady is," David Coleman

told the viewers. *"You get the feeling she's controlling the race the way she wants it."*

The entire ring of spectators in front of the Palace were roaring. As she flashed past the family stand, she just caught a few words of Bernie's song: *"If you wanna be my puppet!"*

She chuckled. She didn't want to be a *puppet!* She didn't want all those early morning runs. Nor all that school work. She certainly didn't want to go to Broom Bank . . ! "So why are you doing this, you ding-bat?" she asked herself. "*Why* . . ? Because if I *win*," she answered excitedly . . . "If I *win* . . !" Something leapt inside her . . . She saw them *hugging* her . . . calling her their little *star* . . . Holding her so *tight* . . . It was such a delicious little fantasy . . . But she was slowing up.

"Starr's *dropping back!*"

"SYLVIA! SYLVIA!" Walter Starr was standing up. His huge, brown-bear fists were clenched. "WAKE UP GIRL! WAKE UP!"

"COUNT, SYLVIA! COUNT!" her mother instructed.

"Something's *up* with that little madam, these days," her father said. "HURRY, GIRL! HURRY!"

"SLOW DOWN, SYLVIA! SLOW DOWN!" Bernie yelled.

She snapped awake and looked at the others ahead. No problem. She knew exactly what she had to do.

"Here she comes again!" David Coleman said. *"You have to admire this style. She makes it all look so easy."*

"Look at that girl, Shaz!" Kevin Button told his wife. "She's like a bloomin' Ferrari!"

"Now *there's* an athlete," Prince Philip said.

"Starr's going to win! YES! YES! STARR WINS IT!"

"I'm betting on *her* for the final, Lilibet," he decided.

She ran to the stand and looked up, expecting *something*

from them . . . but they weren't even looking! They were just *yacking* to Sir Norman!

Bernie pushed her way through and hugged her over the barrier. "You do have a choice, Silly-Sylvie," she whispered. "You don't *have* to do this, you."

"What a race it promises for this afternoon," David Coleman was saying above the*m*. *"Four remarkable athletes. And any one of them is capable of winning it."*

15

The Wishing Race

Monday 28th August

At 2.30pm every seat in the arena was full again and the gates were closed.

At 2.40 the live TV broadcast began and the eyes of the crowd lifted to the overhead screens. David Coleman looked down from his sunny tower. *"We estimate ten million people are tuned in to this event throughout the country,"* he said. *"It really has caught the public's imagination. Her Majesty must be very proud . . . And here she is, out on the track being introduced once more to the four finalists – Four young people who, in their own ways, represent all that is good in the youth of Britain today . . ."*

The row of little Buttons stared at Billy. And at the Queen. And everything! They were absolutely still . . . and silent. Sharon Button, finding herself free, slid her big hand across and took hold of her husband's. "Can you believe it, Kev?" she said. "The Queen of England! Talking to our Billy!" Kevin shuffled across to her. "I wonder where that batty old Jane went?" he said.

"Ober dare! Ober dare!" Bobby told them, pointing across to the finish.

In front of them, Florrie Johansen sucked on an inhaler the track doctor had given her. When the Queen turned and smiled up at her, she almost choked on it. "Now, what's that boy a-tellin' her?" she wondered.

Claire laughed at Hazel trying to curtsy prettily! "Poor old pelican-legs can't bend!" she said. All her teddies were now holding tiny Union Jacks and she'd crossed their legs for luck. Beside her, Pippy had collected some "*See London*" travel brochures and was gazing at their pages as if they were wedding photos. "Oh, Madame Tussaud's Jeff!" she said. "Remember how you posed as John Lennon?"

Walter Starr glanced sideways at Sir Norman and performed what he thought was a warm smile. "Now, doesn't Sylvia look the only athlete amongst them?" he asked. "I mean – look at that cripple boy. You'd never have *him* at Broom Bank, would you?" He pretended that he'd just had an idea. "I know," he said, "when Sylvia's there, we could invite the Queen on a Royal visit!"

Sir Norman didn't take his eyes off the runners. "We could," he said, "*if* she comes. There's the little matter of winning this race first, old boy!"

"Her Majesty takes her seat in the Royal Box," David Coleman whispered. *"And just in behind her, you might have caught a glimpse of William and Harry."*

Hazel stepped from foot to foot, staring at the clean, curving track in front of her. She felt sick and rubbed her hands nervously down her shorts.

Billy grinned at a TV camera and did his trick of pretending to stick a finger up his nose.

Isaac gently let the weight down on his jittering legs and, instantly, the fires began to roll. He gritted his teeth and screwed up his face.

Sylvia was doing groin-stretches. She saw Bernie, at the front again, waving like Mr Bendy! She stifled her laugh and quickly looked away, up into the stand, and began breathing in time to her mother's arm-signals.

When the starting pistol was raised the four of them looked at it, terrified, as if it was a firing squad. They were crouching and slightly rocking . . .

The ten thousand spectators were absolutely hushed. There was just the hum of city traffic.

"ON YOUR MARKS!" Charlie Wilson's voice rang out clearly . . . "GET SET!" . . . His finger squeezed down onto the trigger . . .

The little puff of smoke and the snap brought the crowd to life again.

Billy, Isaac, Sylvia and Hazel jolted forward.

"Here they go!"

Sylvia got away on a breath. BRILL! One-two, one-two, one-two! She couldn't hold herself back this time. Her nerves threw her forward into an amazing sprint.

"It's a good start! Look at Starr!"

Billy remembered what Plod had said and tucked himself in at the back, watching the others. Go on, you poo-heads! Wear yourselves out for little Billy!

Isaac was scampering awkwardly, trying to get his beat right. But he felt all wobbly and disjointed. He *must* get in the lead.

"Now, do you call that running? Honestly!" Walter Starr said pompously.

But when he'd wound himself up to top speed he got that *zoomimg* feeling again. Like he was running right out and away from his pain. "YAH-HAH! HERE I COME!"

"Johansen's going like a ROCKET in lane four!"

"Don't THINK," Hazel told herself. "Just let yourself go!" She was trying to copy Sneezy – the way he just seemed to let his body run its own race. "Think of the hills . . .

Oh, we're at the summit stone. Look at Saddle-back! So clear today!"

"Something's made Fox smile. Almost a lap now. They're coming to the point where they can break out of their lanes, remember. Then we'll really see who's winning."

Isaac pushed down on his Number Sevens like a madman, trying to get to the yellow break line first. He *stretched . . . leapt . . .* telescoped his whole body. He'd never felt this pain before. Nor this new *turbo-power!* "YAH! YOU DEVIL!" he screamed at it. He threw a quick glance back at the others, then cut across them and into the lead.

Florrie sucked hard on her inhaler. Her eyes were swollen and disbelieving.

"It's Johansen! Johansen first, Starr second. Fox third. Then young Billy Button with some way to make up."

Isaac began to sob with the pain. But he laughed through his tears as well because none of them knew his secret. None of them knew the amazing power he was holding back. He could just burst ahead anytime he wanted to. Right away from them. But not yet, Issy. Not just yet you crafty cockney – "YEOW! YEOW! MESS OFF, SATAN!"

The crowd round the back of the sunlit track roared Isaac, Sylvia, Hazel and Billy on. The Queen watched them on the high screen. "He's quite remarkable, isn't he Philip?" she said.

"Oh, he is. But look at the girl."

Sylvia was super-fit. Her training, her preparation, made her run like a real athlete. And she knew what she had to do. She had to *control* the race. Run it at her own pace. Be out in front.

Isaac sensed something was happening. Someone was

coming up behind. Should he use his turbo-pain? Not yet, Issy-boy. Not yet.

Sylvia looked over her right shoulder . . . moved sleekly out amongst Isaac's clattering crutches . . . slipped into a higher gear . . . and accelerated past him.

David Coleman was so excited his voice squeaked. *"Look at THAT! We're looking at a future champion here!"*

Christine Starr was back at the White City Stadium – 1979 . . . the screaming crowd, the excitement, The tension in her stomach . . . She was out in front, controlling the race. "Don't lose it now! Don't lose it now!" she muttered. "You could make the Olympics."

Sylvia's father was *so proud. Now* everyone would see. *Now* they'd know the Starrs weren't like the rest of them.

The Queen raised her binoculars as they came round the bend. Sylvia was racing towards her with a slightly rolling, easy motion. "She looks as though she could run like that for ever!" she told Philip.

Hazel felt herself kick into a higher speed and just go! As if she was riding a motor-bike that suddenly slipped up a gear and raced off with her. "What's going on?" she laughed, her long arms elbowing her out wider.

"What's happening now? What's Fox up to?" David Coleman asked the viewers.

Hazel's legs were thick and her calf muscles felt like hard rubber. None of the others could have run up her hills, none of them. Not even Sylvia ran as far as she did in a week. "YOO-HOO!" she sang out loud.

"She's taking MASSIVE strides now. You'd think she was doing the long-jump!" He stood up in his tower to get a better view. *"She's zig-zagging round Johansen . . . and she's literally PULLING herself past the girl . . . It may be an awkward style but it's certainly effective! Fox has*

taken this race by the scruff of the neck. She could win it!"

Hazel flew past the family stand, towing the others in a line behind her.

Claire screamed, out of control. "YOU BLINKING-DINKING-STINKING HERO!" she bawled. "But why am I crying?"

Florrie Johansen quietly said a prayer. It just came into her head. She didn't know why she said it. "Tek care o' ma boy, Lord! He's in yo' hands now," she muttered.

Christine Starr had run two miles on the spot already! Now she was racing into the Olympic Stadium. The crowd rose to their feet and cheered.

Walter Starr's face twitched and he cursed darkly into his beard. "Sort yourself out, girl!"

The Buttons had had a nice day out. They never really expected Billy to actually *win* anyway . . . but for Bobby, only winning would do. "WUN KICKER, BIBBY! KICKER!" he urged his brother.

"Half-way . . ! It's Fox in the lead, now – just. Then Silky Sylvia Starr. Johansen third – Still looking strong. But way, way behind – you've got to feel sorry for the lad – is young Billy Button. Surely he's out of it now."

Hazel felt full of running.

Sylvia stuck close behind her. She felt okay.

Isaac kept his secret weapon hidden. Just waiting for the right time to roar past them.

Billy began wobbling all over the track.

"Oh, Philip. Poor boy! Poor boy!"

"His legs have gone, Lilibet."

"Button's had it. The pace has finally beaten him."

Billy had one eye on the runners up ahead. He bent low, spread his arms like a plane and machine-gunned a camera "T-T-T-T-T-T!"

"There's only three in it! Button's clowning around!"
But he wasn't.

Plod couldn't believe what he saw on the big screen.
"BILLY! BILLY! PACK IT IN!" he yelled desperately.

Now! They weren't looking anymore. They'd forgotten
him. *Yes! Now! Attack! Attack!* Suddenly, Billy straightened his
body, tensed himself, and started running like he was
running for his life!

*"Would you believe this! Button's come to life again! But
he's left it far too late."*

He could see his school up ahead. "BIL-LY BUT-TON! BIL-
LY BUT-TON!" they chanted. They saw him racing towards
them like an arrow – thin and sharp!

Mrs Bottom dropped her programme in amazement. "Bil-ly
But-ton! Bil-ly But-ton!" she began chanting softly.

"BIBBY WUN! BIBBY WUN! KICKER! KICKER!"

"SYLVIA! SYLVIA! YOU'RE NOT TRYING!"

"Save him, Lordy, save him."

"He's gone past Johansen!"

"Right, Issy-boy! One and a quarter laps left. Time to let
'em have it!"

Sylvia felt the rough boy's elbows as he hurtled past her.
She still felt strong and confident and she chased after him
and followed him past the lanky girl.

*"Button's in the lead! Incredible! And Starr's gone with
him!"*

Hazel wasn't worried. She'd seen Sneezy lose the lead
and still win. She felt so sure that another wave of energy
would lift her and carry her forward again before the finish.
"Relax!" she told herself. "Just let it happen."

Billy laughed and blew a kiss to the crowd. He didn't
know Sylvia was right behind him. Then he started skipping
and singing:

"A daring young man
On the flying trapeze.
He flies through the air
With the greatest of ease."

"Pack it in, Billy!" Plod roared at the screen.

Sylvia was watching. Waiting for her chance. She saw him sort of trip and half miss a step. "NOW! NOW!" she told herself, bursting forwards and sprinting at him. "Quick. Before he sees you!" she gasped.

Billy had lost his concentration. He kind of *felt* these thudding steps behind him and remembered where he was. But it was too late. He heard "One-two-three, one-two-three," close behind him. Then "one-two-three, one-two-three," going past him!

"Oh, top maths group!" he said. "Wait for me, Computer-head!"

"Starr's in front again," David Coleman yelled from the screens. *"But Button's going after her. Then Johansen. Then Fox – last now."*

"One lap left. Perfect!" Isaac thought. *"Now! Now!"* He let the massive pains down for the first time ever. "YE-EE-OW-OWCH!" He felt his whole body jerk as the energy ran through him. And he leapt forward with incredible leaps, almost *flying* after them.

"Johansen's on a charge!" David Coleman gabbled. *"I don't think the others have seen him!"*

Billy gave her an elbow on the shoulder as he pulled past her. Then he heard the clanking of Isaac's crutches on the outside. "Oh, my new knickers! The Iron Man!" he said.

Sylvia grabbed his arm and went by on the *inside!* Billy grabbed at her. Missed. Stumbled a bit. "You old faggot!" he yelled.

Isaac had to swerve to miss Billy's legs. Could he bear this evil pain for the last three-quarters of a lap? "Bugger-bugger-*hell!*" he swore at it.

"Tut-tut! Language!" Billy called after him.

Walter Starr, the big bear, jumped to his feet, elbowing Sir Norman in the face. "I don't believe it!" he spluttered. "She's going to let that *weirdo* go past her!"

David Coleman was amazed. "*He's steaming past Starr as though she's not there! He's timed it perfectly. Only half a lap to go! Johansen's winning!*"

Hazel felt a long way back. But she laughed. She was enjoying it – running loosely, breathing easily, waiting for the burst of speed she knew would come.

A new feeling was creeping into Isaac's body. A really weird sort of numbness. The wicked pains were still shooting him forward but he couldn't *feel* them anymore! It was a great feeling!

"*Johansen's way ahead! They'll never catch him, now. Starr second. Button third. Fox just behind them.*"

Isaac couldn't feel any pain. And he felt as if he was flying. "YEE-HAH! YEE-HAH! I'm cured! I'm okay!" he told the world.

"Glory be to Jesus! Glory be to the Lord!" his Ma sang out, flopping into her seat, her mouth gaping for breath. "This here is a miracle, folks! Yes sir!" she coughed. "Yes siree!"

"CHEAT! CHEAT!" Walter Starr complained.

David Coleman had seen a few things in his time. "*Now, just look at this! Johansen seems to have run right out of his illness! He's in the final straight. The crowd are on their feet! They think it's all over!*"

"I've won, Ma! I've won, Ma!" he screamed, beginning to cry.

Isaac's illness was a disease of the nervous system which had gradually burnt away the nerves of his body . . . He ran for the tape. He just had to look up at his Ma. Their eyes met. They smiled . . . and the nerves into his heart finally snapped and fell away.

Someone suddenly switched the world off. Everything went black. He tumbled down into the blackness.

"Johansen's fallen. Fifty metres from the tape. Right in front of Her Majesty."

He rolled over and over. Then he was dead still. His body a crooked heap.

"Ah-ah-ah-ah-ah!" the crowd wailed.

Suddenly Florrie Johansen knew the truth. "Oh, m' poor sweet boy! Oh, m' poor sweet boy!" she moaned, fumbling for her inhaler and struggling to get up.

The Queen's hands pushed the air, trying to hurry the first-aiders towards Isaac.

Walter Starr couldn't believe his luck. "Don't you dare lose it now, Sylvia!" he threatened.

Sylvia and Billy raced each other to Isaac's body lying on the track in front of them. Sylvia just got there first. She hurdled over it, her feet just skimming a shoulder. It was a good jump. It hadn't slowed her up.

Billy looked down at Isaac and juddered to a halt. He knelt down to him and gently turned his head. "Now, what's that flippin' recovery position?" he wondered, pulling Isaac's knee up high. "No, no – 'A for Airway'. Check his tongue first!" he remembered . . .

But someone yanked at his arm. "Mind the way, son," one of the first-aiders told him.

"Blimey! You were quick! It's not a flippin' first aid race, you know!" *Oh, the race! The race!* "Here I co-ome!" he yelled and roared off like a maniac.

"Button's up again. But Starr's almost there! He'll never catch her."

Sylvia loved it. It was a wonderful feeling. "This must be what it's like to win the Olympics!" she thought. "Everyone yelling – Look at them! The track all to yourself. The tape just there in front! People going bonkers!"

Christine Starr almost screamed. *"She's going to do it, Walter!"*

This was what she'd been waiting for! *Dreaming of! This* moment! She was going to win! She was going to win! Now they'd love her!

Florrie was only half-way down the steps. She couldn't get through the screaming crowd. What were they a-doin' t' her boy, now? A doctor crouched low and plunged a needle into a vein. "Ah-ah!" Mishah gasped, watching everything.

David Coleman was startled. *"What's happening? There's someone on the track!"*

It was *Bernie!* The dumb-head! Sylvia laughed and stumbled a bit. The goo-gonk had dressed herself up like the Queen! A *massive* crown – *Gold card.* A white dress – *Tissue paper!*

"SYL-VIA! SYL-VIA! KEEP GOING!" her father screeched.

Even her guitar had a Union Jack on it! Oh no! – Not our Royal Rock 'n' Roll!

Bernie was strumming and singing in front of a camera:

> *"I'm gonna rock around*
> *The throne with you!*
> *I'm gonna rock around*
> *The royal loo!"*

"Starr's STOPPED! About ten metres from the tape! Whatever's she up to?"

Sylvia laughed at Bernie again and she felt full of fizzy excitement-bubbles. She only felt like this when she was with Bernie. "You *twit,* Bernie! You brilliant, fantastic *twit!*"

"SYL-VI-A-A-A!"

She looked up at him. Then at Bernie. Then at her parents again. And then she started running.

"Starr's off again. PHEW!"

She looked right up into her father's eyes . . . as she ran . . . straight . . . over to Bernie! Then she started rockin' 'n' rollin' and laughing into Bernie's face!

"SYLVIA . . . SYLVIA . . . Oh-h-h!" he moaned.

"Starr's out of it! It must be Button now!"

It was then that Hazel's big spurt of speed arrived. She felt a jolt and began sprinting like a wild thing! Bashing the track with her great legs and elbowing the air frantically.

"Here comes Fox! Can Button hold on?"

"Now come along, everybody!" Mrs Bottom said. She stood there in front of the whole school, conducting them.

"BIL-LY BUT-TON! BIL-LY BUT-TON!"

"HA-ZEL! HA-ZEL!" came from around Claire.

"It could be a draw, Philip."

"Oh yes, Lilibet. A draw."

She was right on his shoulder. She felt her fingers scraping him!

"OUR BILLY! OUR BILLY!"

"HAZEL-*NUT*! HAZEL-*NUT*!"

Four more steps and she'd be past him!

"Oh, it's gonna be Fox! She's going to pass him right at the tape!"

"BIB-BY! BIB-BY! BIB-BY!"

Billy threw himself into the air – launching himself at the tape like a paratrooper.

"Oh-h-h-h! BUTTON WINS! IT'S BUTTON! Is it? YES! Just edging it at the finish!"

16

The Prize

Monday 28th August

Isaac was still laid out on the track in front of the Royal Box. A team of doctors and paramedics were trying hard to save him. Florrie pushed her way between them and flopped to his face. "Oh, Jesus-Lord! Save ma boy! Ma naughty, naughty boy!" she pleaded.

"The pulse has gone! It's gone!" Dr John snapped at the others.

"Out of the way!" one of the paramedics said, beginning to push hard on Isaac's chest.

* * *

Billy lifted the heavy gold cup from the Queen's hands. "Billy and Bobby," she said, "I'm so pleased you won."

Podgers rolled his flabby body over the barrier and out onto the track. He started waddling over towards that crowd round the body.

* * *

Billy turned and held the cup high to the crowd. The roar nearly knocked him backwards. "Blimey, Your Maj, we're a hit, you an' me!"

* * *

The sudden shout for Billy made Hazel look up from Isaac's grey face. "Hey! Tortoise-legs!" Podgers said to her. "I got a surprise for you!" He fumbled a huge bunch of keys out of his pocket and grinned a twisted grin. "We got the ke-eys! We got the ke-eys!" he sang. "We move in to-morrer! We move in to-morrer!"

Hazel looked away. She was beaten.

* * *

Billy was down on the track again, near to all the action around Ice-ark. He plonked the cup onto Bobbo's head and gave him the most gi-normous hug in the world. About a million press cameras flashed and nearly blinded him!

* * *

"But she'd be great in your school, Sir Norman," Walter Starr pleaded. "She's brilliant at maths, you know."

"And she *lives* for running!" his wife added.

"No, no. Out of the question, I'm afraid," Sir Norman told them, watching Sylvia out of the corner of his eye.

Suddenly the crowd boomed with laughter and Sylvia's father looked up at the big screen. *His Sylvia!* Performing to the whole country! With that gipsy-girl!"

They were dancing a sexy mirror-dance they'd only done once before.

> *"If you wanna eat our livers.*
> *If you wanna eat our brains.*
> *Just call an' we'll deliver!*
> *Or send them on by tra-a-ain!"*

Sir Norman coughed politely and inspected his finger-nails. Walter and Christine Starr said the same thing. *"Is THAT our Sylvia?"*

"This young lady is quite a performer," David Coleman told viewers. *"But look at Billy and Bobby Button – hand-in-hand. And here comes the whole family."*

Sylvia's father kicked the seat in front of him so hard it snapped off its legs. Then his big fist came down and smashed through its back. "I'LL GIVE HER `PERFORMER'!" he roared, fixing his eyes on his daughter down on the track. "JUST WHO DOES SHE THINK SHE IS?" He started charging through the seats in a straight line towards Sylvia – like a mad elephant.

"Oh, Walter! *THINK!*" his wife pleaded, scrambling after him.

* * *

"Breathing's gone!" Dr John told the watching faces. Then he pressed his mouth onto Isaac's and blew hard.

"Shit!" Mishah cursed, kicking Podgers, the nearest person to her. He sank to the ground wailing and left Hazel alone.

Florrie Johansen poked Dr John in the back. "Jes' yo' trust in The Great Healer," she said. "He'll save ma' boy. Yo' miserable pill-pushers ain't no use!"

Samuel Rogers lifted his son to his feet. His face looked like a snake's head when he smiled. "Perhaps you'd be kind enough to light the fire before you leave," he said to Hazel's mother. "Archibald and I would like to be comfortable, you know."

Pippy Fox looked confused. "Who's Auntie Bald?" she asked Hazel.

* * *

"The whole Button family is on the track, now!" David Coleman said. *"And young Billy is being swamped by hugs and kisses – There's a popular young man."*

Kevin was zooming around like a racing car – holding the gold cup as if it was a steering wheel. Billy grabbed his Ma's hand and started running with her. "BILLY, ME BELLY! BILLY, ME BELLY!" she complained.

"They're doing a lap of honour!" David Coleman said. *"All twenty of them! No – twenty-one! The Constable's there as well!"*

* * *

Walter Starr jumped the barrier and raced at Sylvia. She was doing the secret handshake with Bernie. "Blood sisters!" they said together . . . She felt a hand clamp itself around her arm. It was almost yanked out of her shoulder! He spun her round and shook her and shook her! She thought her head was coming off!

"YOU LITTLE CHEAT!" he cursed her. "WHY, I'LL . . !"

This was it. You've got to *face him*, Sylvia! Stand up to him! She made herself look up at him. His beard had loads of spit in it! His eyes sort of flashed with white flecks and knives. *Oh!* She looked down. "I – I – I," she began.

"You – You – You, WHAT?" he roared.

"I – I – I . . ." No, Sylvia. No! Come on! You can do it! She clenched her fists, tensed her face and forced her eyes up at him again . . . There! Right into his eyes! The beast! She looked right into him and she shuddered. What a feeling . . . *But she didn't look away!* She just held his glare without moving. Looked right into him. Saw him . . . So that's what you're like, Daddy.

"WHY! YOU! I'LL . . ."

"I'm not afraid of you anymore," she interrupted.

"WHAT?" he boomed.

"I'm just not," she told him, calmly.

"YOU LITTLE . . ." He lifted his great club of a hand.

Sylvia smiled, and stepped towards him, holding her chin up as a challenge.

"WHY, GIRL, I'LL . . ."

"No, Daddy, you won't," she said. "You *can't.*"

She thought he shuddered. His face went all sad and his arm fell to his side. He seemed to be *shrinking.* He fell to his knees, right beside Florrie Johansen, who was praying.

"Oh, Walter!" Christine Starr said. She ran her fingers lovingly through his hair. Sylvia had never seen her *touch* him before!

"The giant has fallen!" Bernie proclaimed. She lifted Sylvia's arm. "And the puppet has come to life! – Hey! *'The Giant and the Puppet!'* It could be an act! I'll be the giant."

"Well *I'm* not being the puppet!" Sylvia told her firmly.

"And now, Her Majesty rises to address the crowd," David Coleman whispered.

The Buttons staggered to a stop and stared up at a screen. "She's got her posh voice out!" Billy told his Ma. "Her Christmas Message voice."

"My husband and I . . ."

"May husband end ay," Billy copied.

"Have great pleasure in granting Billy Button's wish." There was such a cheer he thought he'd been shot! "The Court Order against him is hereby *cancelled.*"

Bobby crossed his legs and held his willy. *Bobbo! No!* Billy thought-warned him.

"Billy and Bobby can therefore remain at home with their *remarkable* family."

* * *

Walter Starr watched them clamp an oxygen mask over Isaac's mouth and nose. The big woman next to him slipped her heavy arm across his shoulders. He tried to knee-walk

110

away but *she pulled him back*. He *hated* it. She felt *warm!* And he could feel her crying.

"Well now, Mr Silver – *Mr Long John Silver*," she sniffed. "Yo' git y'self up outta that hammock, now. D' y' hear?"

What on *earth* was the woman going on about?

* * *

"Billy Button is an example to children everywhere," the Queen was saying. Sharon Button touched her boy's face and kissed his forehead proudly. "We pay tribute to PC Brian Bolt who has devoted so much of his time to helping Billy." Plod came over and shook Billy's hand. "And we must remember Saxham Primary School and their generous love and support." Kirsty and *everyone* were going *bonkers!* Absolutely *boo-bang-bonkers!* He loved it. "And finally we must recognise the help given by Dorothy Bottom, Billy's Headmistress," the Queen said. Poor old Smelly Bottom! She was as red as a tomato!

* * *

A very tall man with jet-black hair had stood up at the back of the family stand. He couldn't take his eyes off a tall girl and a tiny woman down on the track.

* * *

Billy saw Cardboard Jane running at him. She looked like she was gonna BURST! *"I almost had you!"* she shrieked. She tried to belt him one but he dodged and grabbed the Court Order from her hand. He ripped it right up and threw it at her. "Here!" he said. "Stuff *that* up your jumper! Looks like you need something!"

She swiped at him again. "It'd do you *good* in our home!" she hissed.

Sharon waddled between them. "It'd do *you good* in *our* home!" she said, protecting him.

* * *

The tall man decided. *Yes! Do it! Do it!* "Please! Please! Let me through!" he asked the crowd. But they were watching the desperate work of the doctors below. "PLEASE!" he said. He shot another look at the track to make sure they were still there.

* * *

Sylvia and Bernie thought the doctors suddenly looked frightened. "I'm sorry, Mrs Johansen," Dr John said, "but I'm afraid we're losing him. We'll get him to hospital. Make him as comfortable as we can."

"Jesus-Lord! Jesus-Lord! Where are you?" she pleaded.

The wailing siren of the ambulance, as it turned onto the track, made the two girls jump and grab hands.

* * *

He was on the track now. But where were they . . ? Ah, yes. Over there. Talking to that fat boy.

"I'm gonna FART in your room. I'm gonna make it really smelly!" Podgers sneered. The ambulance nearly knocked him over. "An' I'm gonna stamp *crisps* into your fancy-Nancy carpet!"

Hazel just stared at him.

He'd *found them*. At last! He could almost *touch* them.

"Well, it'll be your room, won't it?" she said. "You can do what you like."

"Hazelnut!" he said. *"Hazelnut!"* She daren't turn round. It couldn't be! She was just hearing things!

The Buttons had completed their lap. They stood in a

line, holding hands and watching Isaac being lifted into the ambulance.

Sylvia gently pulled Florrie's hands off the stretcher handle. "Let him go," she said. "They'll look after him."

Florrie laughed down at her boy. "Why, Issy! Yo' no-good trickster yo' . . . I *loves* yo' son! I *loves* yo' so much!" she cried.

Hazel spun round and stared at him. *"Father-man!"*

"Nutkin! I saw you on the telly . . . I . . ."

Someone bashed her in the back and she almost went down! It was Samuel Rogers! Trying to shake hands. "Mr Fox!" he said smarmily. "It was good to do business with you!"

Father-man completely ignored him and gently took her mother's hand. Poor old Mum! Gazing up at him as if he was a film-star! She looked so helpless! Tears just *flooding* down her face. Like an ice-berg was melting inside her. "Jeff," she said.

He stretched an arm out towards Hazel. She tucked herself in and he pulled her close. "Naughty Father-man," she mumbled into his chest.

"Stupid Father-man!" he said into the top of her head.

She felt him bend and kiss her mother a long, long kiss on the mouth. When she breathed out, it sounded like she'd been holding her breath for eight months! "Hello Jeff," she said in her old, calm voice. Her mother was back as well!

"Hello love," he said. "Can I come home? Can I come back to Fell Farm?"

"Excuse ME, Mr Fox!" Samuel Rogers was saying.

"I should never have left. I don't know how I made myself do it."

"Excuse ME!"

"Why did you?" Hazel muttered into his shirt.

"I just had this crazy 'Holidales' idea. That's all I could think about."

"*MR FOX!*"

"You were so excited about it, Jeff."

"But *why* didn't you take us?" Hazel asked.

She felt him shaking his head. "I had to prove," he said, "I had to prove . . . that I could do something by myself, I suppose. Daft, really, now I think about it."

Samuel Rogers was *bursting!* He grabbed Jeff Fox and shouted. "FELL FARM IS NOT *YOURS* TO GO BACK TO! IT'S *OURS!*"

Hazel felt his arm fall away and release her. "I'm very sorry, Mr Rogers," he said. "But I've just phoned my solicitor and informed him *not* to complete the sale. I'm afraid we're *staying* in the house."

Hazel felt her own tears now.

Podgers had gone white and was shaking. "'Snot fair! 'Snot fair!" he bawled.

And, at last, Samuel Rogers crumbled into a person as well. "YOU *CHEAT!* YOU BLOODY *CHEAT,* FOX!" he screamed.

"Oh, dearie me!" Claire teased. "The Humpty Dumpties have had a great fall!"

* * *

"*And now,*" David Coleman announced, "*as Her Majesty departs, it's time for us to leave this rather special arena, ourselves . . .*"

The royal coach waited for the ambulance to pass.

"NOW LISTEN HERE, EVERYBODY!" Sharon Button shouted. "AND YOU, MR BEARDY STARR! Instead of going back to the hotel, we'll get the coach driver to take us all to the hospital – Give that poor woman some help."

17

Death

Florrie had sworn at the doctors and, in the end, they'd let everyone come up to Isaac's intensive care room.

Bernie whispered as if she was in church. "It's spooky-wooky quiet in here, innit?"

Sylvia's eyes were fixed on the green line bleep-bleeping across the screen of the heart monitor. "It's getting so faint, B," she said. "I really liked him, didn't you?"

"Eye-duck tying, Bibby? Eye-duck tying?" Bobby asked, clutching his brother's hand.

Billy was staring at Isaac's grey face. It looked like stone. "Yeah," he said angrily. "If he ain't dead already."

Florrie had stopped screaming. She pulled a pink tissue from the box and calmly wiped his face. "Yo's the stupidest son in the whole wide world," she said. "Did ah iver tell yo' that, boy? Well, it's darned true. Yes, Sirree! The most mad-hoppin' boy on God's good Earth!" Silent tears dripped from her dark brown cheeks. "But ah loves yo', son" – she caught a breath – "more 'n inny mother iver loved her baby-chile! Ah truly do!"

Sharon quietly put a cup down on the bedside locker. "There, dear," she said. "You drink that, now. A nice cup of coffee."

Walter and Christine Starr stood apart from the others, over by the window. He tapped his pen impatiently on the sill and poked at a loose floor-tile with his shoe.

"What's the matter, Walter? What's wrong?" his wife asked.

"Nothing wrong with me! I'm okay!" he snapped . . . But there was something about that big woman that was really troubling him. He didn't want *anything* to do with her. *Nothing!* But he watched everything she did.

Billy stared at Isaac as if he could *make* him wake up.

"It's not *your* fault you know, Billy," Plod said kindly. "And there's nothing any of us can do for him, now."

"I know," Billy said. "But where *is* he? You know – he looks dead don't he? But is he sort of *in there,* somewhere? Can he *feel* anything?"

* * *

When Isaac fell into his blackness he dropped faster and faster – down, down, down . . . as if it would never end. But now he wasn't falling anymore . . . so he opened his eyes.

He was leaning on his Number Sevens by a little gate that led into a garden. It looked fantastic! It was full of a glaring light that made him shade his eyes. And the flowers! They were massive! And the colours! Wow . . . Two huge butterflies settled on his shoulders . . . He smiled . . . clicked open the gate . . . and went through.

* * *

The heart monitor crackled and the bleeping became even fainter. Sylvia looked at Bernie and they grabbed hands.

Hazel stared at the white sheet over Isaac's body. Was it moving . . ? Just.

"Come on, son!" Jeff urged him.

"Hands together and eyes closed," Sharon told the line of Buttons. "Our Father, Who art in Heaven . . ."

Plod stretched over and felt for a pulse. "Very weak. Very weak," he said.

Florrie pulled his hand away. "We gotta *sing!*" she told him. "Sing to the Lord . . !" Her deep voice shocked them:

> *Jesus in the promised kingdom,*
> *Jesus in the land of light,*
> *Lead us from this darkness,*
> *Lead us from this night . . ."*

How could anyone who looked so miserable sing like that? Bernie wondered.

"Now yo' all join in," Florrie told them. They joined hands and began singing and swaying with her.

Walter Starr sort of jolted forward a few steps towards them. He hadn't meant to move at all.

Sylvia and Bernie began a descant, looking into each other's eyes.

* * *

Isaac noticed that everything in the garden was perfect. Nothing had been nibbled or discoloured. It all looked new. Every single leaf was perfectly formed. Every petal looked fresh-painted. And the air trilled with super-clear bird-song. It was great how the birds and animals came right up to him without any fear . . . The only thing that was damaged in the garden was himself! "You old crock, Isaac!" he laughed. "You old cripple . . !" He hobbled around on his Number Sevens admiring it all – as if he'd been invited into a magic palace of wonders . . . "They probably need jes' one ol' thing, broken and dirty," he chuckled.

* * *

Sylvia couldn't believe her eyes. "Look at my father, B! He's gone mad!" she whispered.

Bernie watched him push his way into the line. "What's happened to his face?" she asked. "Something's happened to his face!"

His eyes were glistening and his beard was smiling. Suddenly, he threw his head back and began *singing* with the others . . .

"Jesus in the promised kingdom . . ."

* * *

Isaac came to a wooden bridge across a little river. He hobbled up and looked over the other side. It was fantastic! One massive playground! Full of kids laughing and yelling in the sunshine. Some were riding on the backs of animals – horses, sheep, lions, *dolphins!* Some were dancing to the music of a little band. Some were sweeping through the air on a great swing, shaped like a bird. Some were sitting round a huge table having a feast. They were swimming, building, painting, paddling in boats. And they all looked so happy!

A tall man, wearing a sort of white frock, had seen him and was walking across. "Welcome, Isaac," he said. "Come in."

Isaac looked back for just a moment. The grey mountains looked a long way away, now. Then he stepped down into the sunlit playground.

* * *

Sylvia just *goggled* at her father. They'd finished singing and he was *hugging* Isaac's mother! *Hugging* her! *HER FATHER!*

Bleep . . . bleep . . . . . bleep . . . . bleep . . . . Then *NOTHING!* Just a whistling, hopeless monotone.

"He's dead *now!*" Billy said. The white sheet was absolutely still. "He's just a *thing,* now."

Florrie screamed and shuffled over to him, knocking the locker over. The whole bed shook as she fell on it and smothered Isaac's body with sobs and kisses.

"MOVE!" Hazel told Isaac. "WAKE UP! MOVE!"

"I loves y' boy! Oh, come back t' me, Issy!"

Mishah had found a vase of flowers. She was ripping them to pieces. Swearing. *Crying.*

Plod prised Florrie away from the body. "Come along now, Mrs Johansen," he said. Billy stared at her. She was beating Plod with her fists. Scrabbing. Kicking. "Come along. Come along." It was like a fight in the playground! Sharon wrestled with Florrie's arm, smothering it with softness. Kevin hopped about, trying to grab the other one. Pippy Fox pushed her face into the middle of Florrie's back and cried for her. Jeff had a hand on both of them . . . The whole group, slowly circling, stumbled and staggered across the room . . . and out through the double doors.

* * *

There were two people left in the room.

It was the first time Walter Starr had cried since he'd been forbidden, as a boy. And he couldn't stop . . . Sylvia was staring at him. Shaking her head. Keeping her distance. In all his life, Walter had never touched anyone as tenderly as he did now, his fingers just brushing the boy's face . . .

When he got right up on the bed and knelt over Isaac's body, Sylvia cried out "No! No!" She couldn't *believe* what she was seeing . . . Her father just bent and *kissed* Isaac very gently on the forehead.

* * *

"You don't need those here," the man said, taking Isaac's Number Sevens from him. Isaac laughed. He felt so good. Where was all his pain .. ? For the first time ever he ran free into the playground, skipping and yelling with the others.

It was then that he felt a kiss on his forehead! Who was that? He laughed and looked round . . . There was only the bridge. He ran back to it for a moment and looked over . . . No-one there.

* * *

Inside Walter Starr, something fell to pieces – something he'd carefully held together all his life . . . his stone heart, in which he'd locked away all the love that terrified him. It just broke apart and crumbled. And all that imprisoned emotion flooded out and overpowered him.

* * *

Isaac had run back through the garden to the gate. He was looking at the cold mountains . . . and thinking . . . about his Ma.

He just pushed it open a tiny bit . . . and slowly . . . squeezed through. The laughter of the playground made him turn and look back for a moment. It was like a magic song, filling the air and calling him back.

* * *

Walter Starr charged towards his daughter. Sylvia wanted to run from him! Get away . . ! But she didn't.

He crashed into the end of the bed and knocked a bottle-stand over.

* * *

Isaac shivered in the cold fog. He couldn't even *see* the little gate now. He had scrambled up a stony path and had reached the mountains. He put his cheek against the wet rock-face rising above him and looked up. It was almost vertical! He'd *never* climb *that* . . . Maybe he could just do the first bit . . . He grabbed a sharp edge and dug his toes into a crevice.

* * *

He hit her like a wave and overwhelmed her – folded himself around her. She felt as if she'd sunk right into him. She heard him sort of moan.

"Oh Daddy, Daddy!" she said.

"I'm so sorry, Sylvie. I'm so sorry," he pleaded.

She pulled on him so hard her arms hurt, and she realised, *this* was what she'd always wanted him to do.

* * *

Up and up, higher and higher he climbed. Until the rocks at the bottom seemed to be miles below – straight down beneath him! He imagined falling and quickly looked away . . . He had to lean out backwards and grab the overhang at the top. His hands were sweaty and his feet tingled.

* * *

Sylvia would never let him go! They were making their way over to the double doors and she was clinging onto his arm as if her life depended on it.

* * *

Three-Two-One-*GO!* Isaac let his legs swing out from the rock, into space. Then he began clawing upwards with his feet, trying to get a heel-hold on the crumbling cliff.

* * *

Her father laughed at her and slipped an arm round her shoulders, pulling her closer.

* * *

Isaac got a foot up so that his body was stretched out straight. He felt himself rolling back into space . . . and he kicked and scrabbled at the grass . . . and just managed to squirm himself up . . . and onto the top . . .

He sucked in great breaths and stared up at the white sky.

* * *

They were at the doors now. But Sylvia stopped him and held him all to herself. Just for one more second!

* * *

It wasn't sky, was it? It was a ceiling – a white ceiling! And there was a "bleep-bleep-bleep" coming from somewhere.

* * *

There was a "bleep-bleep-bleep" coming from somewhere but Sylvia and her father didn't hear it. They pushed the double doors open and the others turned to look at them.

Isaac felt okay. He sat up and looked over towards the voices.

Florrie Johansen blew her nose hard and glanced through the doors, for one last time, at her son.

The trouble with miracles is that you're never ready for them!

"Goodbye, son!" she sniffed and turned away. Then she stopped . . . with a jolt . . . and wondered . . . "Mercy-y-y-y!" she sang out. "Am I a-seein' things?" She strained an eye through the door-crack and saw Isaac *dangling his legs over the side of the bed!* "Ya-a-a-a-ah!" she screamed, thundering back into the room.

They all scrambled and tripped in behind her.

"Yo' really alive, boy?" she half-whispered, touching his face carefully. "Is Jesus really a-givin' yo' back t' me?" She began patting him all over . . . "Well, *THE LORD BE PRAISED!*" She tumbled down onto her knees, sobbing a prayer.

"Come on! Let's get outta here!" Mishah ordered him, jabbing his Number Sevens against his ribs.

Isaac laughed at her and stood up, waiting for the pains.

"Don't yo' go an' do too much now, boy!" Florrie said, scrambling to her feet. "I knows yo' tricks. I knows 'em!"

It felt all wrong, standing between his Number Sevens. He know nothing was gonna happen.

It was Bobby who realised. "He was the one who flippin' knew!" Billy said later. Bobbo slipped away from Billy and looked up into Isaac's face. Very, very gently he eased a Number Seven from Isaac's hand and let it slide back against the bed.

Claire looked at Hazel.

"An' niss one," he said.

"Woss the little swizzer up to?" Kevin asked Sharon.

Isaac leaned forward . . . Florrie took a step to catch him . . . and he *walked*. Actually *WALKED* . . . right around her . . . with nice, easy, swaggering steps.

"Flippin' heck!" Billy said.

"Lord be praised!" Florrie gasped.

He *skipped* up to Sylvia, standing hand-in-hand with her parents.

He *twizzled* through the air at Hazel, who pushed Father-man at him!

He *side-stepped* along the row of Buttons!

Mishah smiled at him. *Smiled!* Then she smiled at *everyone . . . and had to wipe her eyes!*

"Where'd y' get y' new pins?" Billy asked him. *Lego-Land?"*

His Ma was coughing like her insides was coming up! And the old bed was rattling and shaking. Isaac ran over and started massaging *her* back. "I was gonna take y' to Jamaica, Ma," he said. "If I'd a'won."

Sylvia felt her father slip away and he marched over to them. "We don't need our money anymore," he realised. "We'll *neve*r send Sylvia away now. *Never!* So . . ."

Florrie's eyes were white and wide.

"I . . ." He just pushed his wallet into her hand . . . "You have it," he said. "Take the boy to Jamaica. Like he said . . ."

Florrie staggered to her feet and touched his beard. "The Lord bless y', mister!" she said.

"Hey! Look at *that,* Sylvie!" Bernie said. "Love amongst the giants!" Florrie was holding him tight.

18

Life

Monday 1st January

It had been snowing all over the country since Christmas Day. Hazel had watched the crazy flakes swirling and dancing. And blocking the track with huge marshmallow snow-waves.

Now it had stopped. And "Claire of the Antarctic" had arrived. And they were getting the dogs out into the yard.

She tried to carry Sneezy over a deep bit but he squirmed out of her arms. And disappeared . . . into a Sneezy-shaped snow-hole, yelping and clawing like a daft puppy!

"Dopey dog!" Claire yelled. And she tossed a snow-grenade at his bobbing head.

The dogs went mad in the snow! Diving in it! Digging! Biting it . . . They laughed so much, they almost wet themselves!

Back in Big Barn they rubbed them down, sat them by the heater and gave them warm broth – just like little kids! She hadn't used her father's yucky food-mix for ages. And she didn't write things in that *Dog Book* anymore, either.

She was doing it her way. It was like she just *knew* what was right for them. She didn't have to *think* about it. Or *plan* it. She just *knew* . . .

She glanced at her new silver cup perched on the beam.

She smiled every time she looked at it – "Best Pack in the Dale". . . She *loved* training the dogs.

"Wanna hear my New Year's Resolution?" she asked Claire.

"What? You gonna give up snogging Sexy Podgers?"

Hazel kicked straw at her. She was really pleased with her decision. "I'm NEVER, EVER gonna run in any more STUPID races!" she said. "Not if I live for a TRILLION BILLION years!"

"Oh, brill! I won't have to sit and watch 'em. And get blisters on me bum!"

"I HATE running races! I'm just gonna run with the dogs."

"Good decision, Super-Girl . . ! And *when* are you gonna show the cup to wonderful Jeff-man?"

She'd been putting it off. The idea had sort of scared her. *"Now!"* she decided. Her stomach lurched. Would he mind that *she had won it?* "What the heck will he say?"

* * *

They were in the kitchen together. At the table. Which was *covered* with sheets of paper! Huge architects' plans. Brochures. Computer print-outs.

"You got *three* rain forests there!" Claire told them.

"What's going on?" Hazel asked.

Her mother showed her a drawing of a family on a farm holiday. "We're going to start a business, Haze," she said calmly.

Jeff smiled at Pippy. *"Together,"* he said. *"Fell Farm Holidays*. You know, Haze. Pony trekking. Feeding the sheep. That sort of thing."

Her mother carefully spread out an architect's plan. "This is Little Barn, Haze," she said. "Look. We're making it into two chalets." Her little hands lovingly pushed it smooth.

"You're *both* gonna do it, right?" Hazel asked.

"*Both* of us," Pippy assured her. "Everything shared . . ." She grinned that playful grin at Father-man — "Like I'll be boss for the *first* fifty years and your father for the *second* fifty. Half-and-half, see?"

Hazel dodged out of the way as Jeff chased Pippy round the table . . . lifted her above his head until she *screamed* . . . then *plonked* her down!

"*You two!*" Hazel scolded, giving them a good shaking. "*Now, sit down!* Both of you! I want to show you something." She looked at *him*. Then at *her*. Then at *him* again. "Now . . ." she said. "I've got something to . . . to . . ." She brought the cup out and placed it on the table between them . . . He stared at it as if it were the *Crown Jewels!*

"*Hazel Nutkin!*" he said. "*I don't believe it! BEST PACK!*"

"It's true," she laughed. "Look what it says — *Fell farm.*"

He shook his head. "I could never have won this, Hazelnut," he realised. "*Never!*"

Pippy took his hand. "Just face it, Jeff," she said. "Dogs are not your thing, are they?"

He kind of twisted his mouth and nodded into the shiny trophy. "No. I'm not a dog man," he said. He looked up. "Not like Hazel-Champ, here! She's a natural."

Hazel laughed and poked him in the chest. "*And,*" she said, "you're not an *adventure-man,* either. You're a *home-*man. A *father-*man!"

* * *

Hazel's leg was *roasting,* so she twisted herself around from the fire. Claire had gone home and a new snow-storm had closed in around the farm. It was the sixth game of their "Everlasting Chess Championship" and she slipped her rook into the corner. "*Checkmate, Father-man!*" she yelled triumphantly, jabbing his shoulder. "That's Hazel-Champ four and Father-Hopeless, two!"

He grabbed at her foot but missed . . . He threw a cushion at her . . . She loved that sort of shiny-happy look he had these days. "Come on. Set them up again!" he said.

"Have we got time?" she asked him.

"We've got all the time in the world!" he told her. "We've got forever and forever and forever!"

* * *

Billy and Bobby stared out of the window at the snow, piled up like daft hats over all the junk in the garden. Billy wanted to *yell!* He hadn't been running for a *week!* A whole *week!* Usually he ran every day. Miles and miles and miles! Being indoors was torture!

"I know, Bobbo," he said. "We could take that present round." Billy had been to Thailand with Plod and the England Boys Athletics Team. It was brilliant! And he'd brought this special present back.

* * *

He helped his Ma to put ten coats and ten pairs of wellies on. She smiled and gave him a hug. He wriggled around, pretending to struggle but she knew he liked it, really. "You all be good," she told them.

* * *

They were like a long centipede, stamping a pathway through the deep snow. Billy led them . . . along the lane . . . . past the shop . . . the pub . . . the church . . . into the estate – full of twinkling, Christmassy windows . . . and all the way to Primrose Close – number fourteen.

"Now, just be quiet!" he told them. His finger hovered

over the bell-push. Then he pressed it and jumped back from the sharp *'DING-DONG'* . . . The door opened . . . and they almost fainted to see her dressed in a *tracksuit!*

"Why! Billy Button!" she said.

"I . . . I've . . . brought you a present, Miss . . . From Thailand."

"Well. That's most kind," she said.

Billy gulped. She don't know what it is, does she! You've made a big mistake, here, Billy Boy! "Open it later, Miss. When you're alone," he said, turning to go.

"Nonsense! I'll open it now," she said, her fingers touching their heads and lining them up to see. "Whatever can it be?" she cooed at the little ones.

Bobbo saw Billy's face and stepped away from her.

She unstuck the paper very carefully and laid it to one side for another time.

Billy tried to join Bobbo but she pulled him back . . . When she lifted the lid off the box, her breathing went all funny. And when she took out the yellow, silky garments she sort of staggered . . . The little ones laughed like crazy and Billy couldn't shut them up . . . And she went as red as Santa's bum!

"Oh dear! Oh dear! Oh dear!" she muttered. "Oh Billy! I . . . I . . ."

They'd never heard her laugh before. Except politely. When she had to. But now, she just bent over and *bellowed* a roly-poly belly-laugh . . ! Had she been magicked into another person or something?

Billy felt better again. "They *are* the right size, Miss," he joked.

She even took all of them indoors for some cake. "Look at these cards, Billy," she said. "From schools all over the country! Congratulating *me* on your win! I feel quite famous!"

Billy began reading them to the others . . . Somehow, he could read these days!

* * *

Back home that night, Sharon Button trudged up the new stairs to the twins' room in the roof. She tucked Bobby in and whispered "Goodnight Bobby-Bo-Bo." She tickled him and he squirmed away into his warm, *dry* bed.

"Goodnight, Mum. Goodnight, Billy," he said.

Sharon beamed as she bent to kiss Billy. "'Night-night my famous champion!" she said. "Happy New Year, son."

Billy knew it would be.

* * *

The stage was so dark! Except for that line of light creeping under the curtain . . . Sylvie listened to the audience-mumble and her stomach *heaved* . . . *"Ready?"* she whispered to Bernie.

"Yeah. Don't forget we're gonna do that *'Me and You'* bit twice."

"I know. And the twizzle."

The music started . . . the curtains *whizzed* open . . . and the floodlights blinded them.

"One – two – three – and . . . *GO!*" They skipped to the front of the stage. Knees up! Big smiles!

First, their mad *"Falling to Pieces"* dance. They'd practiced it a *thousand* times!

Then the song. Everyone loved the "Somewhere . . . anywhere . . . *underwear!*" bit.

Then their *"Copy-cats"* mirror-mime, where they "swapped heads." That was a great hit . . .

The audience loved them . . . and Sylvia just had to look down at the front row. Her mother was clapping like a mad thing! Her father was *WHISTLING* . . . She was never, *NEVER,* going to give up acting.

* * *

After the matinee they drove home very slowly. She loved the way the snowflakes danced in the headlights. When they got out of the car, the two girls grabbed her father's hands and pulled him down the driveway. "Slide, Daddy! Slide! Come on!" she said.

He laughed and did his best to copy the boys he'd watched in the playground.

"You're like a big, clumsy bear!" she said.

"Grrr!" he growled and she screamed.

Something thudded heavily on her shoulder. "Snowballs! Snowball *FIGHT!*" she realised.

Four boys were running up the drive at them, yelling and attacking. Now that the gates were left open, people just came in, all the time.

"Saxons versus Vikings!" her father shouted. "Us four against you four!"

Sylvie scooped up a great ball of snow, crunched it together and threw it at Mopsy. "Dead Viking!" she announced.

"Dead *Head!*" Midge scoffed, splattering Walter Starr on the neck.

Sylvia laughed at her big animal. It was hard to believe people used to be *frightened* of him. At school, it was like they had a completely different headmaster!

"Prisoners! Prisoners!" he screamed with one in each arm. "Into the hill-fort with you two, you Vulgar Vikings!" he said, pulling them towards the house. "It's the coke and cake torture for you!"

Sylvie's mother took her hand and led her in. They

never went running, these days. They sometimes went *shopping*. But they *never* went running.

* * *

Later, Sylvia and Bernie went up to her room to rest, before the evening performance. Bernie flicked the telly on . . . and off . . . Then she got completely lost in a game on the Play Station.

Sylvia wandered around, dragging her fingers over her new, brilliant yellow walls. One of her cut-out dancers had flopped forward so she pressed it back onto the Blu-tac. She liked her room now. And she *never* had to do extra work anymore.

She pulled a curtain aside and looked out at the night. The houses twinkled and winked at her. They looked so *near!* Like she could stretch out and *touch* them . . . She felt like she could just step out of her window and float across the whole snow-covered, sparkling world! She felt *so free!*

* * *

Isaac leaned over the side of the boat and smacked up some spray to make a rainbow.

"Ya-ah, ha-ah!" his six cousins yelled, almost capsizing the boat as they dived into the sparkly ocean.

He *whooped!* "Wait for me!" And plunged in behind them . . . It was brilliant! So clear. So warm . . . He'd learnt how to kick himself right to the bottom like them . . . He followed a shoal of blue, stripy fish zig-zagging over the sand. He loved the way the sunlight wobbled like gold and silver coins on the rocks . . .

Back on the beach they had a tumble-fight on the sand. Isaac won. Then they started baseball. It was great, running free in the sunshine without his old Number Sevens!

"EYE-SUCK!" his Ma called from the top of the beach. "Yo'd better git yo'self riddy! We's got a plane t' catch!"

"Oh, Ma. No!" he protested. He knew that they'd got to go home today. But he'd been pretending it wouldn't happen.

"Yo' jis git yo'self up here, boy!"

"We could hide y', Issy! Cover y' with sea-weed!" Cousin Jo said.

* * *

Isaac stood beneath the big ceiling fan in his cool, white bedroom. For the last eight weeks he'd worn nothing but shorts. He'd swum in them, played footie in them! Everything! Now he had to dress for *London!* He buttoned a white shirt – *with sleeves!* Tied a tie! And pulled on horrible, grey trousers – but *over* his shorts!

When Isaac and Florrie stepped out into Granpa George's garden for the last time, it was *jam-packed* with people. "They could sink the island, Ma!"

"SUR-PRI-ISE!" they all yelled at them. "PARTY TIME, EVERYBODY!"

"Yo' naughty man!" Florrie nagged her father . . .

Later on, Isaac counted *one-hundred-and-forty-eight* uncles, aunts, cousins, *nephews and nieces*. It was just the most *mega-brill* party in the world!

He ate about *six* banana crepes covered with molasses! And he drank almost a bucket-full of pineapple fizz with Jo . . . but then lost the burping competition!

Granma Isabel sang a Caribbean calypso.

Uncle Lucky did his famous coconut juggling.

And Florrie forced Granpa George to tell his old story

about the boat-house again . . . "She looks pretty happy, Jo, don't she?" Isaac said, looking up at his Ma.

"There's a taxi waitin'!" Aunt Hester announced . . .

Isaac had never been kissed so much. "I sh'll miss y', Granpa," he said.

"An' ah sh'll miss *yo'* Issy! Yessir! An mah ol' boathouse'll miss y' too, son. That's the truth!"

He touched the old man's face . . . Those days fishin' with Granpa George were magic! . . "Ma!" he called suddenly. "I'm jus' goin' t' look at the beach! One mo' time!"

"Yo' be quick!" she snapped.

Isaac pushed through the wicker gate onto the top of the beach – the fantastic white beach . . . and he began running . . . He threw his tie up into the clear air . . . he leapt out of his trousers . . . and he tossed his shirt into the beautiful, blue ocean . . . What a fantastic feeling! Running free in his shorts again . . .

* * *

Isaac hid for ages in Granpa George's boathouse. Dropping shells through the floorboards and listening for the 'plop' below. Counting the fish-hooks in the cork. Running his finger over the models they'd carved . . .

When his watch said "18.30" he jumped up. The plane was in the air. He could go back, now.

* * *

As he got near the gate, he could hear the crazy party still goin' on! He just pushed it open . . . a tiny bit . . . and sneaked a look through, searching for his Ma.

"EYE-SUCK! WHY – YO' LITTLE DIVIL, YO'!" she screamed, bustling over to him. She lifted his chin and e him look up at her. "What yo' think yo' a-doin' boy? akin' us miss that plane, an' all!"

"I don't know, Ma. I don't know what I was doin'." He dropped his head. "I jus' . . . I jus' . . ."

"Yo' jis figured yo' could stay here alonga us, is that it boy?" Granpa George asked him gently.

Isaac looked up into the old, creased face. His eyes felt tickly and warm . . . "I jus' . . . I jus . . ."

"Well thas what you're gonna do, Issy!" Granpa George announced. "An' mah b'loved Florrie. Yo' jus' gonna live right here alonga us! We all decided!"

His Ma was *laughin'*. An' *noddin'*. An' *cryin'*. "Is that okay, Issy!" she asked him. "Would y' miss ol' London? Tell me the truth, now, boy!"

Isaac looked around. Everyone was laughing and shaking hands. Ruffling his hair. Punching him. Jo had got the baseball bat again . . . Jamaica was so *bright!* So *skitty!* Isaac knew he was really gonna *live*, here.

The End